Where I Found My Heart

Natasha Hughes Smith

Published by Talking Stories with Natasha

Email: authornatasha@yahoo.com.

Copyright 2024 Natasha Hughes Smith

Paperback: ISBN 979-8-9889770-3-2

Cover Design: Crown Designs

The people and staff at the airport were moving way too slowly for Cassie. She was accustomed to the hustle and bustle of a big city. After graduating from the University of Michigan a decade ago, she accepted a position at an acquisition company in New York and she worked there ever since. It was the type of job that took her around the globe and back again. As a valued employee, she had the option of working remotely and had returned to Michigan to live. She had seen the most sophisticated of cities, so she hated jobs that took her to small towns with slow-moving people. She was tempted to shove a few out of the way at the airport.

When she finally got her luggage, retrieved her dog from the cargo hold, and found the rental car office, there was no one to be found; nothing but a sign that read "be back soon".

"Ain't this a bitch!", fussed Cassie.

Cassie stared at her beautiful dog, Princess, a Goldendoodle with the shiniest red coat. Her fur was as soft as it was luxurious. She fussed some more, but only the walls and Princess could hear her as she tapped her fingers and complained while looking at her cell to check the time. Princess whined in response to Cassie.

"I know girl. I hope we can get to our rental home soon.", Cassie comforted Princess and petted her head. "Hello! I need to get a vehicle before it gets dark! Damn!", shouted Cassie to the security camera mounted on the wall.

The last thing she needed was to be out in the dark trying to find her way to the small town named Raymond; it was the closest town to her true destination, Staton, Mississippi, with an appropriate Airbnb. She could have stayed at one in Staton, but she did not want to be that close to the Staton family while she snooped around. The business trip was not getting off to a good start, she thought, she hoped that was not a sign of what was to come. It felt like she had been waiting for thirty minutes, but it had only been five. She took out her phone once again and decided to call her best friend.

"Hey, girl!", sighed Cassie.

"Well, hello, Money Bags.", teased Michelle.

"Yeah, right Micki! The money is the only reason I took this assignment. The payout will be huge if I score this one. I might even be up for a promotion, then I'll really be Money Bags.", laughed Cassie.

"You sound tired. Get some rest and I'll call you tomorrow morning to check on you.", suggested Michelle.

"Rest? Girl please, I have not even checked into the rental house yet! I've been waiting *forever* for the attendant to return to the car rental office. They had the nerve to put up a *be right back* sign. Shit, I'm tempted to check out my own car!", laughed Cassie.

"I know you're fucking lying!", exclaimed Micki.

"Bitch, I wish.", sighed Cassie then whispered, "Here comes this lazy MF now. I'll call you later."

Cassie's anger boiled and she examined the attendant from head to toe before she spoke.

"Do you *work* here?", questioned Cassie.

The attendant took a deep breath; she hated dealing with out-of-towners with attitudes. She could tell that this one thought she was *something*. The attendant returned the scrutinizing stare at Cassie's Urban African Bohemian style. Cassie wore a pair of tan faux suede leggings and a tan high-waisted G-string bodysuit; the bodysuit was sleeveless with a mock neck. Cassie's jacket was a pseudo-ethnic print kimono with shades of orange and brown that

4

she paired with tan fold-over cuffed leather 4-inch heeled dress boots. Interesting thought the attendant, until she noticed Cassie's nipples; the heifer doesn't have on a bra.

Cassie noticed the attendant's look of disapproval deepened and she assumed that she noticed her oversized nipples protruding beneath her bodysuit. Cassie never wore a bra and didn't believe the uncomfortable things were necessary especially since she had perky double-D's. Her mother and Auntie always warned her that she'd better get used to a bra's support because soon gravity would have its way. Cassie posed with her hands on her hips and one well-toned leg extended as if ready for a photographer.

"Yes, Ma'am. I'm Laura. How may I help you?", she asked.

"Laura, I'm here to get the Range Rover I reserved.", informed Cassie.

"What's your name or your reservation number?", requested Laura.

"It's under Cassandra Williams.", Cassie provided.

Laura pecked and pecked as she made an odd noise indicating that something was wrong.

"Is everything okay?", asked Cassie, already well passed annoyed.

"We don't have any Range Rovers. Looks like the system defaulted you to a Honda SUV when the Range Rover wasn't available.", Laura sighed.

"Wait a minute. Repeat!", insisted Cassie.

"It's not available. I'm surprised you wanted a luxury vehicle anyway since you have a dog...", Laura supplied.

"Princess is accustomed to luxury.", smirked Cassie.

"Are you sure about that?", questioned Laura.

Laura smirked as she pointed to Princess standing over a puddle of urine.

"Princess! Where is your diaper? My God! This would not have happened if we hadn't waited an hour for you!", Cassie accused.

"Ma'am, it wasn't an hour and I don't want to argue about it. So, you want the Honda or not?", asked Laura in her gentle Southern drawl.

"This is not acceptable! I need the supervisor.", insisted Cassie.

Cassie began digging through her carry-on bag for napkins to wipe up Princess' mess.

"I am, Ma'am.", Laura informed.

That's a lie, thought Cassie.

"Just give it to me. I'll see about changing it later. I do not have time for this!", fumed Cassie.

Princess started whining as if coming to Laura's defense.

"Don't you start.", sighed Cassie as Princess sighed as well in unison.

Cassie stomped to the parking garage, and Princess trailed behind her. Everything about the car was wrong and the more she noticed things the angrier she became. She was furious that she and Princess had to make do with the smaller vehicle, but she was too frazzled to fuss with Princess about it. She needed to focus on the GPS app on her phone because the model she was forced to accept didn't have advanced features. After missing her exit and rounding back, she finally made it to the Airbnb and she hoped there were no hiccups with it and the maid would arrive on time the next day. Not having maid service would ruin everything and she would be unable to focus on her job if that happened. She knew she was in for a challenging work assignment when she spoke to the owner of Staton Farms, Mrs. Staton. What a bitch, thought Cassie, but she had to remind herself she would be too if someone was trying to convince her to sell something she held dear.

Carrying the burden of fighting off the acquisition company should have been the job of the controlling partner of the ranch, but Momma Staton, as the younger ranch hands called her, did not want her son to deal with it. He was so laid back, just like his father; God bless his soul, thought Pink Staton. She hoped that arrogant Ms. Williams would not call her again, but she knew, like clockwork, the young woman would. She looked at the letter for the tenth time; she could not believe the arrogance of it all. She had not wanted her son to know about the letter, but it would have been disrespectful not to share it since after all, he basically inherited everything from her husband.

"Pooh Bear!", she shouted as she poured her coffee and then walked to the breakfast table.

Her eldest entered the dine-in kitchen to the delicious aroma of breakfast as he had done his entire life. His mother had insisted and promised as a young bride to always cook breakfast for her husband and their children. She didn't grow up with as much wealth and prestige as her husband, KC Jr. had, so she wanted to keep some traditions of her childhood. Seeing her mother cook a huge breakfast always made her feel loved as a child and she wanted to provide those same memories to her own.

"Good morning, Ma." Don't you think I'm a little too old to be called Pooh Bear, Pink?", he leaned in for a kiss, "Everything looks and smells good as usual."

"Okay, KC.", laughed Pink, "You know I do not like my first name."

"And you know I don't like mine either.", commented KC.

"Well, we both should understand then, but the difference is that you were named after two great men. You ought to be proud.", scolded Pink.

"I am, but I just want to be recognized as my own man and judged by my accomplishments.", KC informed.

He leaned to kiss his mother again, this time on the forehead and she nudged him away.

"Fix your plate and have a seat. We need to discuss this letter we received yesterday.", insisted Pink.

He obeyed his mother, but he didn't think that the situation warranted as much time and energy as his mother was putting into it. She shoved the letter into his hand after he sat at the table.

"Read it!", ordered Pink.

His mother stood with her hands on her hips as she waited for a response. KC quickly glanced at the first paragraph and then turned the paper face down on the table.

"Well ...", Pink scoffed.

"Okay, and?", KC commented then nibbled on his toast.

"They are trying to force us to sell. It says this is the highest offer and the longer we wait the lower the offer. They are plotting something, but what, I do not know.", snapped Pink.

"We are not going to be intimidated or bullied. So, relax Ma.", KC informed.

"You are so much like your sweet father. It took him forever to get upset about anything, but when he did ... heads rolled, baby!", Pink declared.

"Let's hope it doesn't come to that. I don't like to get angry.", advised KC, "If I were you, I wouldn't give the letter another thought."

"It's hard not to when I know their representative is going to call, yet again!", Pink fussed.

"You can let me speak to them.", insisted KC.

"No, no. You have more important things to do.", suggested Pink.

"You're right. I'm going into town then later meet with the staff to discuss some improvements I want to implement.", drawled KC.

"Okay, you do that. I'll deal with the bitch!", fussed Pink.

"Ma ... Is that necessary?", KC commented more as an instruction to calm down than a question.

Cassie was so thankful for a restful night's sleep; she was quite energized. She was pleased that she could make coffee, eat an energy bar, and have her morning call with her bestie. She had also called the car rental office and gave them a huge piece of her mind. Enough, that they agreed to provide a full-sized Mercedes SUV for the price of the Honda. She shocked herself that she was able to negotiate that deal; she planned to parlay that energy into a victory over Mrs. Staton. Next up, she would take Princess for a walk after calling Mrs. Staton to discuss the letter that had been delivered by a courier service the other day. She prepared herself mentally because Mrs. Staton was a stubborn bitch; she reminded her of herself if she was honest.

"Here it goes.", Cassie said when she pressed the call button, "Hello, Mrs. Staton."

"Speak of the devil!", greeted Pink, "I was just telling my son earlier this morning that you probably would be calling."

"It would be nice to actually speak to the man in charge and not a representative or secretary.", Cassie sneered.

"He's much too busy handling important and relevant business to waste time on this.", snarled Pink.

"I see. We need a decision now or the offer will continue to drop over time.", informed Cassie.

"I don't know what type of business owners or people you are used to dealing with, but we are not desperate for money nor have we ever been!", snapped Pink.

"The ranch is not bringing in the profits that it used to; it's a money pit basically.", Cassie informed, "But perhaps you actually haven't *seen* the profit reports.", Cassie accused.

"I don't know what type of math you are doing, but it's not adding up. I'll say this before I hang up on you. We do things a little differently down here compared to New York. We keep this ranch running not just for money, but for the local folks. We want to make sure that they have quality and healthy food. Everything isn't about money. We have several other businesses for that! Good day!", Pink concluded.

"I know this bitch did not just hang up on me. This job is going to be harder than I thought.", sighed Cassie.

Cassie slouched down on the sofa; she realized that Pink Staton was a true challenge and adversary. She was going to have to try a different approach since a strong arm and intimidation wouldn't work on her.

"Hey, Princess! Let's go for a walk, maybe you can help me clear my head and brainstorm a new strategy.", suggested Cassie, "And maybe by then our upgraded car will be here".

"Woof!", barked Princess.

Cassie took that as agreement and got up to retrieve Princess' leash. Since the pair would be in town for a few months, she decided there was no time like the present to start exploring.

"Come on girl! It's gorgeous out. It'll be nice to walk around.", insisted Cassie as she attached the leash.

The thing Cassie knew she would enjoy about her time in Raymond, was the fresh air as she stood on the small front porch and inhaled. Since they had arrived at night, she couldn't see the quaint beauty of the home, but in the light of day, she thought it was adorable. It was a mock cape cod ranch with white-washed brick along the base of the home with soft grey vinyl siding on top. Spring flowers and rose bushes trimmed the house all around from front to back. A picture-perfect scene like that one made Cassie feel it would be nice to take a jog or long walk with Princess every morning. That was the only thing a girl could get used to about these parts, thought Cassie, but she was not the only one excited about getting out.

"Hold on, girl!", fussed Cassie as she struggled to close the door.

Off Princess ran the moment she heard the door slam. Princess knew that sound very well; it meant it was time to go. Cassie was just as excited as Princess, although she would never admit that to anyone. They had been jogging for thirty minutes when Princess caught sight of a rabbit; she was determined to introduce herself to the strange creature. Cassie struggled with the leash, but Princess' drive was too strong for both Cassie and the leash. The leash snapped and Princess was able to run at full speed; the goldendoodle disappeared from her sight.

"Princess! Oh, my God!", cried Cassie.

She frantically called and ran toward the direction Princess had sprinted, but the dog was nowhere in sight. Princess was too over-stimulated to hear Cassie's cries or even to notice the pick-up truck approaching as she attempted to dash across the street. Guy pounded his horn and the brakes praying that he would not hit the beautiful dog that seemed to be misplaced in the woods. His dog,

Boy, barked his warnings as well; the fur of the black and white Scottish Collie moved with each bark and excited motion.

"Thank God!", sighed Guy, "Sit tight Boy!"

He hopped out of the truck immediately to calm the poor beauty who was startled by his blowing horn and then his dog who was barking from the passenger seat.

"Hey, gorgeous. It's okay. What are you doing out here, girl? You're much too pretty and fancy for these parts.", Guy proclaimed as he surveyed the area.

His ears perked up when he heard the frantic cries of a woman; her accent didn't sound like she was native to the area. She was no doubt the mother to the fancy goldendoodle, thought Guy.

"Leave my dog alone! You better not steal her!", shouted Cassie.

Princess wiggled to release Guy's gentle grip on her collar and ran toward Cassie to beg forgiveness. Cassie was in tears and could barely see the man whom she had accused of trying to steal her precious angel.

"Ma'am, I was trying to calm your dog. I was inches away from hitting her when she dotted out in front of me chasing a rabbit. I would never steal anything. I'm sorry if I frightened you.", Guy explained.

Cassie wiped her eyes and could see the stranger more clearly now. He was the most striking man she had ever seen and that said a lot since she wasn't into white guys. However, something was commanding about his stature, yet his voice and mannerisms were comforting. He was a working man, a man good with his hands; his hands looked weathered and muscled like the rest of his six-foot-five frame. He looked every bit of the Southern farmhand with his work boots, jeans, and flannel shirt. The only thing that would have separated him from a man from any decade in the twentieth century was his modern luxury pick-up and his manbun. She wondered just how long his hair actually was.

"I'm Guy. You are?", he asked, but didn't get a response, "Ma'am?"

His eyes questioned the peculiar stare of the fancy woman with the fancy dog.

"Oh, sorry. What did you say?", asked Cassie.

"Nothing. I just wanted to make sure you and your little Princess are okay. I can give you a lift back home.", informed Guy.

"Princess ...", Cassie uttered.

She went into her city-girl defensive mode yet again.

"I saw her ID tag.", Guy explained.

He could see that she was distrusting and why should she be when she was out in the middle of nowhere with a stranger? He didn't want to make her feel any more uncomfortable so he excused himself.

"Well, I'll be on my way if you two are okay. You might want to keep her on a leash around here.", Guy informed.

"Yeah ...", Cassie dismissed.

She quickly tied the leash in a knot around Princess' collar and ran off. She didn't have time for the stranger's mansplaining things to her, but if she had to listen to one mansplaining, he would be a good one to whom to listen. His voice was warm like a soothing bubble bath and burning candles after a long day of work.

"Refocus girl!", Cassie whispered.

Cassie hoped that she could remember her way back. After a few twists and turns, they finally made it back to their original path. At that point, all she wanted was to get back to the Airbnb and give Princess a quick bath before she went into town to explore.

"Boy, I feel really bad. I hope they make it back safely. She didn't even tell me her name.", confessed Guy.

Boy whined in agreement and then laid his head on Guy's lap.

"Well, we couldn't force them in the truck. I'll have to trust that the good Lord will protect them.", sighed Guy, "Who knows we might just run into them again. Wouldn't that be nice?"

"Woof, woof.", Boy agreed.

Guy almost missed his turn; he couldn't forget the caramel beauty. She wasn't like any of the women in his hometown or even in college. She had a very artsy sophisticated style and he loved her wavy hair that she had in a bun atop her head. He imagined her letting it down and him running his fingers over its softness.

"I'll take you into town after we swing by the cabin. Sound good?", asked Guy.

"Woof.", responded Boy.

"My Boy!", laughed Guy then rubbed Boy's head.

Chapter 2

The car rental staff had delivered the luxury SUV and drove the other one off while she was chasing after Princess. Cassie had followed their instructions and left the key inside the vehicle. She was relieved that the company had accommodated her as she hadn't wanted to go into town looking like she couldn't afford the best. Although she didn't know anyone there, appearances were everything; especially with her coming there for the sole purpose of securing Staton Farms. Who would take someone seriously who drove up on the property with the same type of car as one of the hired help, she thought?

"Let's see how Raymond looks.", Cassie announced, "Ready Princess?'

Princess followed Cassie to the kitchen island to check out the brochures she had noticed upon their arrival. Princess stood on her hind legs as she sniffed the brochures on the countertop before Cassie picked one up. Cassie was eager to see what Raymond had to offer, but every brochure was for Staton. Is there nothing to do here, she thought. She removed her cell phone from her designer belt bag and confirmed that all the night spots and shopping were in the nearby town of Staton.

"That's what I get for assuming, Princess. Looks like we have a bit of a drive to do. Ready?", asked Cassie.

"Woof", Princess barked.

Cassie led the way with Princess on her heels. She opened the back door for Princess to hop inside. As Cassie settled in the car, she opened the brochure so that she could enter the address in the GPS feature of the car. Princess began to pant; it wasn't taking long for the temperature to rise. It was much warmer than a Spring day in Michigan. Cassie lowered the back window so that Princess could stick her head out. It was a gorgeous spring day; the air seemed so fresh to Cassie. She was glad that her Airbnb was not far from the downtown Staton area since it was located just on the outskirts of both towns. As they entered the city limits, she was surprised by the beauty of the courthouse, a southern Greek Revival. She had no idea that Southern architecture was so grand other than old plantation mansions she had read about or seen on television.

Cassie had second guessed on bringing Princess to town, but she was glad to see others with their fur babies. It appeared that the shop owners were receptive to allowing them to enter the stores; so, she could freely take Princess in to explore as well. She spotted a sign that indicated public parking and was excited to see that it was free. Free parking was like an apparition where she came from; especially when she lived in New York. If you thought you saw free, you'd come back to see a ticket on your windshield. This was a whole new world to Cassie. She pulled into a parking spot and was eager to see what the town offered, but more importantly to find out what the locals knew and thought of the Statons. She would use any rumor or dirty laundry about the family against them. She couldn't wait.

"Come on, girl! Let's check things out.", Cassie giggled.

Cassie didn't understand why she was so excited, but she felt giddy and so did Princess; Princess' tail flickered back and forth faster than she had ever seen. Cassie locked the car and the two headed around the building to walk along the main street. The two seemed to take a deep breath simultaneously as they leisurely window-browsed and people-watched. Pets inside one window caught Princess' attention and she dragged Cassie to the entrance.

"Okay, girl. You're overdue for a new toy.", laughed Cassie.

Cassie allowed Princess to take the reins and she followed the beautiful dog inside the pet shop. The shop was small, but it had every toy, dog treat, and food you could think of. The owner seemed to be really big on natural treats and food. There was so

16

much for Princess to sniff and explore that she didn't know where to begin.

"Hello, Miss. Please let me know if I can help you find what you need.", greeted the cashier.

"Thank you I will. Hold on, girl!", giggled Cassie as Princess pulled.

Cassie noticed an adorable toy and an interesting healthy dog food brand name, Staton's Pride. Cassie wondered if it was the same Staton family that had the bitch, Pink, at its helm; interesting she thought. Then suddenly as she was trying to grab a bag of dog food, Princess pulled away when she heard the bell jingle over the entrance.

"Princess, don't act like you have no home training.", fussed Cassie.

Cassie rushed to the front of the store only to find her Princess lapping it up with the stranger and his dog.

"That a girl. You're so cute.", gushed Guy over Princess.

All while his dog was running in a circle after its tail; one would have thought Princess truly was a princess.

"Why are you running to strangers? Come here.", fussed Cassie.

Princess completely ignored her and continued to lick Guy's face like he was her long-lost daddy.

"Woof!", barked Princess.

Princess' expression suggested that Cassie should be there doing the same; Cassie could not help but smile. She took in the tall stranger all over again; this time she saw him thoroughly. His bright blue eyes were mesmerizing and demanded that her eyes devour him. His thick wavy blond hair was pulled tightly into a manbun like she remembered. His muscled arms were ready to rip

17

through his shirt, and the veins on his hands were pronounced as he gripped Princess possessively like she was his. Cassie quickly imagined those same hands laying claim to her body. Both Guy and Cassie were lost in their thoughts.

Guy could smell Cassie's fragrance caress his face as if God himself blew his breath gently over her frame. Due to the excitement of their first encounter, he hadn't noticed anything other than her beautiful face and hair until then. He allowed his eyes to freely gaze upon her. She wore trendy sportswear; the grey pants and tank top hugged her as tightly as he would have wanted to hold her. Her tiny waist, full hips, and buttocks cried out to be touched and caressed. Even her perky breasts and large nipples taunted him, but she stood bold and not concerned that her nipples were protruding through her tank. He was accustomed to more modest women so he wanted to turn his gaze away, but he was transfixed.

"Howdy! I was hoping to see you again. I was worried that you wouldn't find your way back.", confessed Guy.

"As you can see, all is well. We are fine.", laughed Cassie.

Cassie waited to discover his true agenda. From the looks of him, he didn't make much money and might be looking for a sugar momma; a gullible woman from out of town, she thought.

"Yes, you are indeed. You ladies are both an incredible sight for sore eyes. Right boy?", announced Guy.

Boy howled in agreement with Guy then trotted to Cassie and stood on his hind legs to greet her.

"Boy! Oh, my goodness. You are adorable and a big boy!", laughed Cassie, just like your fine daddy, she thought.

She rubbed his head and Boy tried to lick her hand.

"I'm Guy.", he greeted and extended his hand, "And this is my dog, Boy."

"Nice to meet you. I'm Cassie.", she provided and accepted the strong handshake.

She glanced at his strong hand as it held her petite one and was about to smile when she noticed the dirt under his fingernails. It was an instant turn-off and she abruptly pulled her hand away.

"Don't let me keep you. I'm sure you need to get back to work.", Cassie informed.

The cashier, Guy, and even the dogs looked at her oddly. The cashier chuckled at the city girl and then turned his attention to his inventory list.

"That sounds oddly familiar ...", chuckled Guy.

He thought about how his mother often dismissed him when she disagreed with his advice. Despite her resistance to anything he said, he was compelled to say something to continue their conversation.

"You are the most beautiful woman I've ever seen.", confessed Guy, surprised that he voiced what he felt the first moment he saw her.

"Where the hell have you been? Your head must have been up a cow's ass not to notice there are a lot of bad bitches out here. Sounds like some bullshit to me. My dog.", Cassie demanded with her hand extended for the leash.

Guy did not know how to respond to her comment and decided to ignore it and do as he was told.

"Sure.", Guy affirmed, "Bye my little Princess.", then he whispered in Princess' ear, "The queen has spoken."

Guy laughed as he handed the leash to Cassie and she stood there as if waiting for him to obey her command. He awkwardly looked at the tickled cashier and his confused dog then turned on his heels and left. He wasn't even able to complete the business he needed to address with the cashier; yet he felt compelled to obey the bossy out-of-towner.

"Come girl, let's purchase that toy you were eyeing. And we might as well try this Staton's Pride dog food.", Cassie instructed.

Guy stared through the window as he walked toward his truck. Cassie was so bossy, that he wondered if she ever let her guard down and relaxed. Perhaps she just needed the right man to handle the job and he would make it his mission to do it before she slipped away and back to where she came.

Cassie carried the small bag of dog food and toy to the counter. She thought it was no better time than the present to ask the cashier if he knew anything about the Staton family.

"I'd like to get these two items. Is this dog food by the same family that owns Staton Farms?", Cassie inquired.

"Sure is. You must be new in town.", the cashier concluded.

"Yes, I'm in town for business.", offered Cassie.

"I figured. Otherwise, you'd know that the Statons are Staton Mississippi. They own the farm and their family developed the town two hundred years ago.", he educated.

"Really?", Cassie questioned.

"Yes, ma'am. They are *really* good folks. Even going way back.", he informed.

"Really?", laughed a doubtful Cassie, "Not racist at all?"

She hoped that from one Black person to another the cashier would be honest and not try to save face for the rich Staton family.

"Three generations of my family have owned and run this business; the Statons have been our biggest supporters. My

20

grandfather was good friends with the great-grandfather of KC Staton III. ", the cashier beamed, "Like I said, really good folks!"

Well, that was a strike out, thought Cassie, maybe someone else would be willing to spill the tea on the family and discuss their dirty little secrets. Cassie nodded and thanked the owner for his customer service and left hoping that she could strike gold later that day elsewhere. Princess spotted Guy and barked, but he was too busy laughing with an elderly lady in front of the bakery to pay any attention to Princess.

"Damn it! Why does he have to be standing in front of the bakery? It would have been nice to get a treat.", moaned Cassie.

Princess seemed to understand exactly what Cassie wanted and needed as she tugged the leash toward the bakery.

"Oh, no. We don't need to run into them again.", fussed Cassie, "You must want to have Boy's pups and me to hook up with Guy! No and no; that's not happening!"

Princess whined as she obeyed Cassie and followed her direction to the opposite end of the street. Cassie didn't want to get sidetracked by anything, not even a handsome man like Guy. She reminded herself all she had to do was picture his fingernails, which would squash any chances of that ever happening. She grimaced and continued her walk toward the other shops. She spotted a shop called Nicknacks and Patty-Wacks.

"Let's check out this shop, Princess. I probably can find some souvenirs to take back home.", suggested Cassie.

Princess reluctantly obeyed her mom as she glanced backward down the street at Guy and Boy who had finished their conversation and was headed in their direction. Cassie was drawn inside the store as Princess had been to the last one. She spotted something she thought was perfect for her Auntie Gloria.

"Good day, Ma'am.", greeted a blonde Southern bell.

"Hey!", greeted Cassie and then pivoted to the trinket in the window, "This is so beautiful!"

"Yes, it is. It's one of the pieces from the collection of a local designer and crafter, Ms. Rose.", the cashier informed.

"Oh, wow. Do you think I could order a custom piece?", asked Cassie.

"Perhaps, but it's rare that she has time for that with her hectic schedule. I can find out if you ...", paused the cashier.

Jill, the cashier, lost interest in the discussion when she noticed Guy staring through the window. She tossed her hair in hopes that he had been staring at her unaware; little did she know that Cassie had captured his attention yet again. Cassie turned around to see who or what had stopped the young woman in mid-sentence. Not you again, thought Cassie as Guy entered the boutique.

"Hello, Guy. Don't you look mighty hot.", Jill said and then cleared her throat, "Would you like a cold bottle of water to cool off?"

Cassie noticed the flirty body language of the store clerk and the ridiculous smile froze on her face. Hey if dirty nails do it for you, go for it, she thought with a smirk.

"I'm good Jill, appreciate it though.", Guy smiled.

How could she not have noticed his teeth before, Cassie thought, maybe she had been too focused on his body. His teeth were perfect and whiter than any she had seen; they elevated him from ruggedly handsome to model good looks.

"Hello again, Cassie.", beamed Guy.

"Are you following me?", Cassie accused.

She refused to make it obvious that she was warming up to him; a bit more than even she was willing to admit to herself.

Princess had no problem whatsoever letting him and Boy know that she was excited to see them.

"No, not at all.", laughed Guy, "I'm much too busy for that."

"Busy?", laughed Cassie, "That's what you call it. It looked more like loafing and talking to people to me."

"If you must know, I had company business to take care of. I work on a local farm and I swing into town from time to time to check inventory.", explained Guy.

"Really?", expressed Cassie.

Well, that explains the fingernails she thought as she stared at his dirty nails.

"I know, I look like I work strictly with my hands.", chuckled Guy as he eyed his dirty fingernails.

"Uh, yeah.", laughed Cassie.

"Well, that's what I prefer, but sometimes the boss wants me to take care of the stuff she doesn't feel like doing.", Guy explained then switched topics, "I see you are going to let Princess try our dog food."

"You work on Staton Farms?", questioned Cassie.

Her interest suddenly skyrocketed and peaked; perhaps he was her way to get some inside information that she could use against the bitch.

"Practically all my life!", laughed Guy, "But that's enough about me and definitely enough about Staton Farms. Ms. Jill, do I need to replenish any inventory here?"

"No Guy ... but you could help me out with a box. It's much too heavy for me to lift.", suggested Jill.

"Sure thing.", offered Guy.

"It's the big box right at the stockroom door.", Jill informed.

Cassie doubted very seriously that Jill needed help; she figured Jill just wanted to prolong Guy's visit and see him flex his muscles. Guy returned carrying the bulky box; every muscle in his arms, back, and chest was flexing almost ripping the shirt apart. She understood completely why Jill was so determined to see the show. Cassie's and Jill's eyes followed Guy's every movement as he bent at his knees to lower the box to the floor safely. Oh, my God, thought Cassie as her eyes devoured his thick muscled thighs that seemed to be as clear to her as if she had used x-ray vision. Jill began to fan and then gulped down a few drinks from her bottled water.

"Oh, goodness Guy. I don't know what I would have done if you hadn't stopped by.", Jill sighed as she fanned her face with a sheet of paper.

"Jill, you know I do what I can.", Guy smiled then turned his attention to Cassie, "That's why I have to look out for Ms. Cassie here. She's from out of town."

"Man, please. You are way older than me. Cassie will do just fine.", Cassie corrected.

"Yes Ma'am.", laughed Guy.

Cassie cut Guy another annoyed look for that expression as well.

"When are you going back?", asked Jill.

Jill and the other ladies in town did not need any more competition; it was hard as it was to get Guy's attention.

"I'm here for work; so as long as necessary to get the job done.", informed Cassie.

Trust me I don't want your dirty nailed man, thought Cassie, no matter how fine he is.

"Speaking of getting the job done, I need to swing back by Carl's shop. Someone and their pretty dog distracted me while I was there.", laughed Guy as he tore off a sheet from Jill's notepad, "Cassie, please give me a call. I'd love to show you around or tell you about some of the local restaurants."

Cassie accepted the paper, any other time she would have crumbled it and pitched it to the trash as she often did when men provided unwanted attention, but she could put up with an evening or maybe two with Guy if it meant getting the dirt on his boss.

"Well ladies, I'd better get a move on it.", informed Guy.

Boy followed Guy out of the store, but not without one last lick of Cassie's hand and a sniff of Princess.

"Happy?", whispered Cassie to Princess as she snuggled her face, "Jill, can you find out if the artist can make two more of the glass figurine I was looking at?"

"Sure, will do. Can you jot your name and number down for me?", Jill suggested as she slid her notebook toward Cassie, "Any friend of Guy is a friend of mine. He has a great sense about folks."

"Ok ...", giggled Cassie, "I can tell you are crushing on him and I'm not trying to step on any toes."

"Ms. Cassie, Guy is the hottest ticket around here! He is as kind as he is fine! He comes from a good family; he is honest and hard-working. A girl can't want anything better than that.", Jill announced, "So if I were you, I wouldn't be so quick to toss him aside."

"Thanks for the tip, but I'm not you.", laughed Cassie, "I have other options a whole lot higher on the totem pole than that one. Bye."

Cassie continued to laugh as she exited the building. She hoped other townspeople would not be as assumptive to think that she would lower her much-deserved high standards just to have a man. Guy, be he fine, was nothing like any man she ever considered dating and she didn't see the need to start now.

"Well Princess, I think that has been enough excitement for you. I think it is time to go home and let you sample this Staton's Pride and don't gobble it down just because Guy works there.", informed Cassie.

"Woof.", barked Princess.

Her eyes seemed to imply that she would never do something so tricky.

"Yeah ... you love that man for some reason.", pondered Cassie.

As long as Princess was alive, she hated every man Cassie dated. Cassie's mom, Gina, said it was because Princess could sniff out a man up to no good. Cassie eyed Princess, you drank the punch just like everyone else in this town, but I don't have time for distractions, she thought.

Chapter 3

Cassie had been in the small country town for a week and she had surprisingly settled in nicely. She liked taking the short drive into town for supplies and found it heart-warming that people remembered her. All of that she planned to use in her favor when it came to collecting dirt on Pink Staton. She had been so engrossed in her surroundings that she hadn't checked in with anyone back home. Her friend's incoming call reminded her of that.

"Hey Cassie, have things gotten better?", asked Michelle.

"Yes, Micki, thank God. I don't know what I would have done if I had to keep that smaller car!", informed Cassie.

"Have you done any sightseeing?", asked Michelle.

"We've gone into town multiple times and walked around their quaint downtown. That's all.", informed Cassie.

"Good. I know you are there for work, but you really need to let your hair down while you are there and have some fun. Especially after what you went through with Jaquan!", insisted Michelle.

"Girl, please don't talk that devil up! I am so glad to be done with him. He *really* had me fooled! Claiming to be a community activist and owning a successful business...", sighed Cassie.

"Right, a business he was looking for a sugar momma to bail out of debt. I swear, if you hadn't left him, I was going to kick his ass and then yours.", laughed Michelle.

"Girl, right! I would have deserved that ass beating.", laughed Cassie, "He's one of those "fake it till you make it" type of brothers. His favorite saying was that he mastered the ghetto. I do not have time for that shit."

"I feel you. Speaking of men, are there any sexy men there?", asked Michelle.

"Girl!", laughed Cassie, "If you listen to the townspeople there is."

"Okay, bitch! Tell me about him.", ordered Michelle.

Cassie laughed at her friend's excitement and expected them to laugh more when she told her about Guy.

"So, there's this guy, everyone thinks is so incredibly kind and handsome…", started Cassie.

"Ok, I'm feeling it… What's his name?", anticipated Michelle.

"His name is Guy. Like did his mother run out of names or wasn't excited about his birth.", laughed Cassie.

"Guy … okay?', laughed Michelle.

"This joker almost ran over my Princess! That was our first encounter.", supplied Cassie.

"Shit! Is my girl, okay?", asked Michelle.

"Yes! I was going crazy looking for her and there she was licking and loving on the man who almost killed her.", laughed Cassie.

"No, Princess! You can tell she's not from the streets.", laughed Michelle, "Her expensive ass!"

"Right! After that, wherever we went in town, there he was. It was like he was stalking me.", emphasized Cassie.

"Are you hiding something? Tell me how he looks.", laughed Michelle.

"He's …", paused Cassie.

"Spit it out! Damn!", fussed Michelle.

"FINE AS HELL!", blared Cassie.

"Woof!", howled Princess.

"Okay, bitch! That's what I'm talking about!", laughed Michelle, "So why was that so hard to say?"

"Because he's white.", confessed Cassie.

"Okay and?", questioned Michelle, "Have you had any good luck with other guys?"

"Shut up!", laughed Cassie.

"Exactly! So, it's time for a change. So how does he look? Is he a bookworm or businessman type?", inquired Michelle.

"Far from it. He's six-foot-four.", Cassie began.

"Ooh yes!", shouted Michelle.

"Muscular with thick arms and thighs. You know I love a thick muscled thigh!", sighed Cassie, "His shirts look like they are about to rip off his body."

"Ooh girl, yes! I can see the sex now. He can toss you on the bed and rip off your clothes.", moaned Michelle.

"Oh, Gees, do all of that when we get off the phone.", Cassie complained then continued, "He has the thickest and waviest blond hair I've ever seen that he pulls into a man bun."

"A man bun?", questioned Michelle.

"Yeah, girl.", sighed Cassie.

"I can dig it though. What else?", begged Michelle.

"He has the most gorgeous smile and gentleness in his tone and is so welcoming… He's a rough and rugged type, yet there's something underneath that I haven't pinpointed yet.", concluded Cassie.

"He sounds like *everything*! I hope you let him tap that ass while you're there.", Michelle persuaded.

"I don't know how I feel about the man bun and his dirty nails.", Cassie huffed.

"Dirty nails? I was wondering if he worked on a farm from your description.", Michelle offered.

"Yeah, he does, in fact on Staton Farms. He gave me his number to hang out sometime; so, I'll use that opportunity to drill him about his employer.", informed Cassie.

"Fuck that! You better use him for some nasty sex!", ordered Michelle.

"Girl, closing this deal is more important than getting laid. Besides I can't get past the dirty nails.", insisted Cassie.

"That's what soap and water are for. I better not hear about his nails again. He probably had just come into town from the farm.", suggested Michelle.

"Yeah, he implied as much.", Cassie provided.

"You better not toss that fine tall glass of water aside. You need a good fuck!", laughed Michelle.

'You ain't never lied. I truly do.", laughed Cassie, "Maybe I'll give him a call and make plans."

"Yes, make it make sense! Don't let your Auntie Gloria hear that you are passing up a *good* man.", giggled Michelle.

"Exactly. I don't need her to go into some long-drawn-out story about one of her friends that passed up good men and almost ended up alone with only her nice possessions to keep her company at night.", chuckled Cassie.

"Changing topics, it seems you must still be running into a brick wall on this current project.", concluded Michelle.

"Yeah, everyone in town thinks the Staton family is wonderful. Even a Black shop owner said that his grandfather was best friends with the great-grandfather of KC Staton III. I just knew I could dig up some racist shit about them, but I'm coming up empty-handed.", confessed Cassie.

"All white families are not bad, even the rich ones. Well, you might have to try a different tactic.", Michelle cautioned.

"Perhaps, but I think they are just saying nice things because I'm new in town. I don't trust it or that bitch Pink Staton that I've been dealing with.", admitted Cassie.

"Wait a minute! I thought the head of Staton Farms was a man... that KC Staton you mentioned earlier.", remarked Michelle.

"Yeah, he is, but his mother Pink is taking over and refuses to allow me to speak to him. She says she's handling the situation and he's much too busy to be bothered with me. Even when I call their offices directly, everyone sends me to her voicemail. I don't know if he's incapacitated and runs it in name only or what.", claimed Cassie.

"Wouldn't that be something if you pulled KC and you two started dating.", laughed Michelle.

"It would be more like a miracle; that pit bull of a momma is guarding him like crazy. It makes me wonder if I would have better luck with him.", laughed Cassie.

"Do you know what he looks like?", asked Michelle.

"Nope. I cannot find his picture anywhere on their website. Just his name is listed, but everyone else has a photo.", explained Cassie.

"Wow! You could have run into him around town and not even know it. Damn. Well Sherlock, please have fun while you are investigating and the next time, we talk, you better have been shagged by Guy or even KC!", laughed Michelle.

"Whatever! Bye, girl!", laughed Cassie.

Cassie had spent so many years focused on her career and denying everything else, a love life and a social life. She treated men much the same way as most of them treated women; she used them for her sexual needs and that alone. She never listened to the warnings of her loved ones; they often warned her that she needed to make time for the important things and truly experience life. However, when she did let her guard down, she met Jaquan and that was a mistake she vowed she would never make again. She'd wait until she was fifty to try again if that's what it took to meet the right man.

Similarly, Guy had tunnel vision concerning his work, and few women had an appeal strong enough to change his gears.

"Guy! Hello! Where is your head?", shouted Pete.

Guy leaned leisurely on the white wooden fence surrounding one of the barns. He had been standing in the same spot for who knows how long. Since meeting Cassie, he found himself getting distracted and thinking about her. He regretted that he didn't ask for her number instead. He would have taken her out by then if he had.

"Sorry, Pete. My mind was miles away. What's up?", questioned Guy.

"I see. What's weighing so heavily on your mind; is it the rumors of an acquisition company trying to take the farm?", inquired Pete.

"No, even though it should be. That's not in my job description.", laughed Guy.

"It's not, are you sure? I thought nothing was done around here without your approval. You're second in command around here, aren't you?", teased Pete.

"Am I really though?", laughed Guy.

"So, what is it? Don't tell me the great catch of Staton and Raymond Mississippi has his heart stolen by a Southern Bell?", teased Pete.

"Far from it. It's actually a Northern Bell. Do they call them that?", laughed Guy.

"What? About time! What's special about this one? You've passed up some *hella-good* catches before. Did she play the damsel in distress like the rest of the ladies after your heart?", joked Pete.

"The total opposite!", laughed Guy, "She'd probably save my ass before she would allow me to save hers."

"Oh, wow another Pink Staton. You admire aggressive women that are like your mother, don't you?", teased Pete.

"What can I say? I am my father's son. An independent woman gets me off.", laughed Guy.

"So, when will you bring her around to meet me and the other guys? That would be fun?", Pete asked.

"I have to take her out on a date first.", uttered Guy.

"You've got to be shitting me! You haven't gone out and you're already daydreaming about her.", Pete laughed.

Pete's boisterous laughter almost made Guy feel embarrassed and hated even more that he hadn't asked for her number.

"Fuck off.", groaned Guy.

"She must be the one. When has the mighty Guy ever pined for a girl?", laughed Pete, "I got to tell my wife about this!"

"Why did you stop by? I have work to do.", fussed Guy.

"I was just doing you a favor and drove around the property to keep an eye out for anything unusual.", informed Pete.

"Well, I think the county Sheriff could be making better use of his time.", Guy insisted.

It was a clear hint that Pete's time was up and that he had aggravated Guy to the point of wearing out his welcome.

"I get the hint. I'm just looking out for my best friend and his life's work. Hopefully, this new lady friend can give you something else to focus on.", Pete bellowed as he walked away, "What's her name?"

"Cassie. Now get the hell on!", shouted Guy.

Try a different tactic, the words of Michelle had been running through Cassie's head since their conversation. She sat in the cozy living room of her Airbnb sipping her second cup of coffee and pondering what to do. She decided that maybe she would present a slightly smaller offer to Pink Staton to consider; perhaps Ms. Staton would think she had exhausted her ideas. She could play the long game with this one and revisit this project by suggesting yet another division for the Statons to sell off until there was nothing left but the farm. Cassie had other deals that she could close by phone in the meantime to keep her productivity numbers up.

Cassie looked at the portfolio of Staton Holdings and spotted one that was just small enough to fit into her plan; she would propose that they sell their black walnut tree business that consisted of acreage well outside of Staton and for that matter outside of Staton County entirely. Next, she would focus on the food company.

34

"Here it goes.", Cassie announced to Princess.

Princess whined at the announcement.

"Okay, I promise I will call Guy today too! Geez!", Cassie fussed.

Cassie hesitantly dialed her opponent. Ms. Staton must have memorized her number and was refusing to answer, she thought, when finally, Pink answered the call.

"What now, Ms. Wiliams?", demanded Pink.

"I think it would be an excellent idea for us to meet in person. I would love to run one more proposal by you.", suggested Cassie.

Pink thought it was unnecessary and a waste of time to meet in person, but if Cassie wanted to waste her time and money to come to Staton so be it.

"My schedule is quite tight. When were you thinking?", questioned Pink.

"I can make flight arrangements to be there tomorrow.", lied Cassie, "I was hoping we could meet at 2 pm at the Staton Community Center. I checked with them this morning and they have a small conference room available."

"That will be fine. I can squeeze you in before my 4 o'clock meeting.", confirmed Pink.

"Thank you. I'll see you tomorrow.", Cassie provided.

"Yes ...", uttered Pink then disconnected the call.

Pink couldn't figure out what scheme Cassie had up her sleeve, but she knew it was some sort of trick.

"I'm ready bitch.", declared Pink.

KC entered the room and frowned as he heard his mother speak negatively.

"You must be talking about that acquisition lady ...", decided KC.

"Forgive me, I don't like to use that term about other successful businesswomen, but she has definitely earned it.", laughed Pink, "How is your day going, Pooh Bear?"

"Better than yours from the sound and look of it.", chuckled KC.

"Wow, it shows, huh?", asked Pink and KC nodded his agreement, "I really shouldn't let her get to me. Especially since I agreed to an in-person meeting tomorrow."

"Oh, she's coming to town. Are you meeting here?", inquired her son.

"No, way! I do not want her snooping around our land. We are meeting at the community center in town.", Pink notified.

"Should I go along to referee?", laughed KC.

"Who's fighting?', asked Tim as he entered.

"Tim! Hey man!", greeted KC and hugged his long-time friend.

'It's been too long, Tim.", scolded Pink.

"Sorry, Momma Staton. I won't stay away so long the next time.", pleaded Tim.

"Where is Henry? Why didn't he announce you?", inquired Pink.

"I told him to let me surprise you both.", informed Tim.

"Well don't just stand there, come here and give me a hug!", urged Pink.

"Yes, Ma'am.", chuckled Tim as he playfully jogged over to hug her, "So do I need to join your son and protect you from this person who wants to go toe-to-toe with you?"

"It's just a damn acquisition firm, RQ Acquisitions. We have a meeting tomorrow at the Community Center.", informed Pink.

"KC, why aren't you handling that?", Tim inquired.

"Perhaps, if you weren't calling me by my father's name, I would tell you.", joked KC, "If you must know Ma insists on letting her handle it. It gives her an excuse to be tough and stubborn."

"She doesn't need an excuse for that!", laughed Tim, "That dude is in for a fight on his hands."

"Thing is, it's another stubborn and aggressive woman. They have really been going at it. I've never heard Ma refer to another woman as a bitch until this lady.", informed KC.

Pink felt awful that her son had heard her utter the word, but she couldn't find any other word more suitable to use.

"Oh, a catfight! Maybe I should tag along.", laughed Tim.

"I don't plan on going that low with her, but if she attacks first, then it'll be her last time.", laughed Pink.

The three laughed at the idea of the two powerful women fighting and the mayor having to rush in and break it up. KC was about to add to the story when he received a call. He looked at the caller's ID; he decided to step out before answering.

"Excuse me. I need to take this call.", KC announced.

KC walked briskly from the family room to accept the call.

"What do you think that is about?", asked Tim.

"I don't know. He's never wanted privacy from me, not even as a teenager.", Pink reflected, "I swear if that Ms. Williams went against my instructions and contacted him ..."

"Calm down. You know that he wouldn't disrespect you like that and he definitely wouldn't allow someone else to.", Tim reassured.

Princess howled and howled until Cassie dialed Guys' number. Cassie swore that Princess was more human than a dog and seemed to understand everything. Cassie gave in to Princess' demands and nervously dialed. She had never been nervous or unsure around any man and was not about to start now. Get it together Cassie, she thought.

"See Princess; Guy is not answering.", Cassie whispered.

She felt silly for even calling the man and even more so for giving into the desires of a dog who really didn't voice a desire for her to call. Cassie was about to disconnect the call when Guy answered.

"Hello, may I speak to Guy?", asked Cassie.

"Yes, this is he. Is this Cassie?", asked Guy.

He immediately regretted asking if it was her. She would know he didn't get any calls from other women, but maybe that was a good thing, he thought.

"Yeah, it's me.", awkward thought Cassie, "How's it going?", Cassie asked.

"Great, just another day on the farm. You?", asked Guy.

"Just another day in the life of a boss chick, making deals, negotiating deals ...", laughed Cassie, being turned down by boss bitches, she thought.

"I am so glad you called. I should have taken your number instead...", began Guy.

38

"Well, you've got it now.", laughed Cassie, "I was wondering if you wanted to hang out tonight. You promised to show me around."

"Yes, I did. I would love to hang out and get to know you.", confessed Guy.

"Hold your horses, cowboy. I agreed to you showing me around, nothing more.", Cassie corrected.

"Yes, that was the original plan.", Guy began, "I know the perfect little restaurant to go to. Do you like seafood?"

"Only if it's fried.", Cassie laughed.

She had no desire to go anywhere fancy with him; she didn't want to take the chance of running into Pink Staton at a fancy restaurant. Who am I kidding, thought Cassie, he was a farmhand and could not afford fancy and she would end up paying for both checks out of guilt.

"Great! Can I pick you up?", Guy asked.

"Sure. You can pick me up at 6 pm. I'll text you the address.", informed Cassie and then disconnected.

Normally, she always insisted on meeting a guy at the date location; however, this time she'd do things differently. The townspeople loved him, so she felt assured of her safety, and if he tried anything she always carried a knife in her purse or pocket. Besides, sharing a ride would offer her ample time to see how much information about Staton Farms and the Staton family she could obtain.

"Cassie, Cassie, Cassie.", whispered Guy.

Guy believed getting to know a woman like her was the ultimate challenge. He thought it was nothing more powering and enticing for a man than to have a woman who had it all, intelligence, determination, and a strong will, but was open to surrendering her trust and being completely vulnerable to him. He knew that when he finally cracked the code for Cassie, her love would be intoxicating. Instantly, he panicked about what to wear. She needed to see that he wasn't the filthy farmhand that she seemed to assume he was.

"Well, Princess, you got your wish after all. I'm going out with Guy tonight.", laughed Cassie as Princess howled and then licked her face, "It won't be all fun and games. This is still work. I bet he knows some dirt on that rich bitch."

Princess whined at Cassie, was there any hope for her owner? Cassie gently pushed Princess aside so she could find the perfect outfit to wear. Even though it wasn't a *real* date, she wanted to be so sexy that Guy would tell her anything.

Pink was very concerned despite Tim's reassurance that she had nothing to worry about, but as far as she was concerned the last thing the farm needed was KC speaking to Ms. Williams. Her son had a big heart and she could see him trying to make it a win-win for Ms. Williams and the farm, if he thought she was nice. Pink wanted there to be one stand-alone winner and that should be Staton Farms. She noticed that KC jogged past the entrance of the study toward the stairs as if he were dodging her. No, you don't, thought Pink.

"KC!", shouted Pink, she thought that should get his attention, "What is going on? Where are you rushing off to?"

"Ma, I don't have time right now. I have an appointment that will change everything for this family!", proclaimed KC as he jogged up the stairs.

Pink was frightened; this was not the time for him to take control or initiative, especially when she had Ms. Williams' back against a wall.

"Please, God, don't let my son bring everything crashing down.", prayed Pink.

Chapter 4

Guy had butterflies in his stomach as he stepped out of the shower. It had been a while since Guy had put as much time and effort into his attire as he did for his first date with Cassie. Nor had he felt as much hope for anything; there was surely something special about her. He rummaged through his closet for what he hoped would make a statement, so she would know there was more to him than what she realized without him having to broadcast it to the world. He spotted his navy-blue jeans with white-washed running down the thighs and whiting at the knees. They had thick tan stitching down the sides with tan cotton along the top of the side pockets with gold-tone rivets. The back pockets displayed an upside-down tan fleur de lis with the same tan cotton trimming the buttoned flaps.

Guy held the pair up for scrutiny; he had to look his best if he wanted any attempts to soften the strong-willed vixen to be successful. He searched his shirts until he found a tan short-sleeved with a tapered waist. The up-rolled sleeve of the shirt and the inside of the placket had colorful paisley prints in gold and blue with gold-tone buttons.

He pulled the jeans over his thick thighs and muscled buttocks then put on his shirt making sure it was neatly tucked inside his jeans. He slid a thick three-pronged tan leather belt through the loops and buckled it snuggly over his muscled physique. The shirt barely contained his muscled chest and arms; the buttons strained against his chest. He brushed up his long wavy blond hair that dangled to his mid-back and swooped it into a bun. He returned to his attached bath to view himself in the mirror and sprayed on some cologne.

"Well, *cowboy*, this better work.", chuckled Guy remembering Cassie's nickname for him.

He adored Cassie's voice and her sassiness as he remembered her calling him a cowboy. He instantly thought of the one thing he knew she hated and examined his hands. Perfect, he thought, not a trace of his hard work left from the day, and the only thing left to do was to put on his watch and his boots. Guy removed his designer wooden link watch from his dresser and walked inside his closet to get a pair of boots. He had decided to wear his short-stacked heeled tan ostrich leather boots with a low shaft that would fit perfectly under his skinny jeans. The round toe of the boot when paired with his clothing selection, gave him more of an urban aesthetic than a country one.

Cassie, like Guy, wanted to make a lasting impression. She wanted to render Guy speechless without looking like she had put a lot of effort into her look; she wanted it to be sexy but at the same time like she threw something on at the last minute because she didn't care. She giggled as she pulled her soft boho off-the-shoulder knitted sweater from the drawer. She pulled the cream sweater overhead and grabbed her light blue skinny distressed jeans. She slipped on the mid-waist jeans over her thong-covered buttocks. She looked down and laughed again as her nipple attempted to slip through the knitted sweater.

"Mommy would have a fit if she saw me!", laughed Cassie, "Oh well, if he sees a nipple, all the better."

Fortunately, it was a thick loose-fitting sweater so she should only have a few instances of a peek-a-boo nipple, she thought as she walked over to the bed to retrieve her shoes and jewelry from her luggage. She spotted her long brown boho leather necklace with a round fringed disk that resembled a dream catcher; she paired that with matching leather tassel fish hook earrings. Next, she slid her small slender feet into her embellished beige 4-inch heeled strapped sandal, and then, she walked inside the adjoining bathroom to view herself in the full-length mirror. Something is missing, she thought, then she decided to remove the rubber band so that her soft brown naturally curly hair would fall down her back. She bent at the waist, ran her fingers through her hair to fluff it, and then stood to gauge her appearance.

"Perfect!", giggled Cassie as she turned in the mirror and looked over her shoulder to view her derriere then shouted, "I'm about to leave girl. How do I look?"

Princess dashed from the living room to the bathroom and barked her opinion. Princess jumped on Cassie's leg as she barked and wagged her tail.

"I take it I have your approval.", laughed Cassie, "Now get down girl. I don't want to smell like you on my date. Speaking of ..."

Cassie walked to the dresser to spray on her favorite designer perfume that was sure to grab Guy's senses then she retrieved her small Fendi beige hobo bag with the name in gold-tone metal letters.

"Okay, girl, that must be Guy pulling up. Wish me luck!", giggled Cassie.

Guy took several breaths and checked his nails a second time before exiting the truck. He didn't want anything to spoil the evening; there was something strangely overwhelming about the date as if their entire lives were riding on it. As he approached the door, Cassie opened it before he could knock.

"Let's go.", insisted Cassie.

She flung the door closed and switched past him leaving her enticing aroma in her wake.

"Hello...", laughed Guy as he talked to her back and inhaled her scent.

Guy chuckled as he had always sensed that she was forever trying to maintain control, but he hoped that she would relax enough to get to know him and allow him to know her. It was as if

Cassie could read Guy's mind and hear Michelle at the same time saying relax. Michelle's words were more like relaxed and get fucked, thought Cassie with a smirk. She decided she would try to be less aggressive and wait for him to open the car door. Guy turned around and sprinted to the truck not knowing if she would open the door without his assistance or not. He was surprised that she was waiting impatiently for him with her hand on her hip. If the dog was Princess, then surely Cassie was the Queen. Guy opened the door for Her Majesty.

"After you, my Queen.", Guy declared as he bowed to her.

"So, you have jokes tonight.", laughed Cassie as she struggled slightly to climb into the truck.

She normally would have insisted that she didn't need any help, but without asking permission his muscular arms gripped her effortlessly and eased her onto the seat. She touched his forearm without thinking and felt its strength and thickness and then his cologne intoxicated her. Seemingly out of her control, she kissed him and smoothed the hairs on his nape into his bun. Maybe she was ready to be shagged after all, she thought, as Michelle had jokingly put it.

Guy was shocked by her actions; he had hoped for a kiss, but he thought he would be the one initiating it. He was not accustomed to sexually aggressive women, but for Cassie, he could get used to it. He blushed as he closed the door and gave Cassie one of those dazzling smiles, she had come to find so sexy. I do believe you will get a special treat tonight cowboy, thought Cassie. Guy slid into the driver's seat and fastened his seatbelt.

"You look stunning.", admitted Guy.

"Thank you. You look pretty good too, cowboy, and your whip. This is a really nice truck. What kind of truck is it?", Cassie complimented.

"It's a 350 GMC Siera Denali Ultimate. I just got it a few months ago.", Guy explained.

"I didn't know that farm employees have it *this* good.", Cassie commented.

"Thanks, but I don't know if most do.", Guy said hesitantly with a chuckle.

"So, where are you taking me?", asked Cassie.

"There's a quaint and down-to-earth spot, a bar and grill, in Staton I'd like to show you. It's named Silverbacks.", Guy informed.

"Silverbacks? Like the gorilla?", questioned Cassie.

She wasn't feeling the spot and the crowd she assumed would be there.

"Well yes ... but mostly like the older men who always want to have power over others and control people.", chuckled Guy, "There are a lot of wanna-be silverbacks in the area."

"Interesting ...", Cassie uttered.

"Pete, one of my friends, owns the spot. He comes from a wealthy family with a controlling father and he rebelled against his father every chance he got- from his women to his line of work. Pete is the Sheriff of Staton County and owns a few businesses in the area.", Guy informed.

"Well, I do like a good bar and grill; especially if it has a pool table or darts.", laughed Cassie.

"It has both. Do I sense a hint of your competitive nature?", teased Guy.

He knew full well that she was aggressive at everything and tonight he had no doubt she would be that way romantically too. He was ready to be dominated and beaten by Cassie that night, but not literally Guy smirked at the thought.

46

"Yes, all my life. I ran track in high school and college. I had a full ride with my academic and sports scholarships combined.", Cassie beamed.

"Looks like we have sports in common. I played a little football in high school and college as, a defensive end. No scholarships to speak of, though.", chuckled Guy as he noticed her shocked expression, "Looks like you weren't expecting to hear that I attended college."

"Well, no ... I never thought about it.", confessed Cassie.

No, why would she think a farmhand had a degree, she thought, then she paused and realized that she had made that assumption as well; he had never told her that he was a farmhand. The two continued small talk as they listened to an oldies but goodies country station that played her grandmother's favorite song by Reba McEntire. He noticed that she was tapping her fingers.

"Do you know this one?", Guy asked.

"Yeah, my grandmother loves country music and would play this one a lot whenever I visited her.", explained Cassie.

"Where is she from?", inquired Guy.

"She grew up in Tennessee and moved to Michigan after high school as a newlywed.", Cassie disclosed.

Cassie then realized that she was failing at her original task; she was supposed to be drilling him for the scoop on the Staton family and not sharing her family history. She abruptly changed the topic.

"Ever since I came here for a job assignment everyone has been bragging about the Staton family and how much they've done for the community. Is it all true?", Cassie questioned.

"For the most part ...", Guy admitted.

Oh, here we go, that's what I'm talking about thought Cassie, I might actually find some dirt on Pink Staton.

"What do you mean?", Cassie asked.

"Well ... good people try to make good decisions that benefit everyone, but you can't please everyone. Especially when they're a rich family; they are bound to make deals that benefit their family more than others. Right?", suggested Guy.

"True ... so did the Staton family make a deal that hurt someone.", questioned Cassie.

"It just depends on who you ask...", Guy paused.

"So, what is this KC about? I don't hear people talking about him and he's a big shot of Staton Farms. That's strange, don't you think?", questioned Cassie.

"I think people like him well enough.", Guy commented.

"Don't you think it's odd that you don't see pictures of him anywhere, only ones of his mother?", Cassie inquired.

"I don't know what you mean. But maybe he's laid back and since his father died, he allows his mother to run the business while he manages the farm because that's what she always wanted to do. That's the rumor anyway.", Guy added.

"It's got to be more than that. I mean what are the Staton streets saying? Are there any illegitimate children running around?", joked Cassie.

"Why would you be interested in that?", Guy remarked at the odd questioning.

"Who doesn't like to hear gossip?", laughed Cassie.

"Around here the most important stories are those of resilience and people pulling together no matter their background or wealth. We are all family around here. Back in the day when the world around us was filled with hatred and bigotry, we took a stand against that shit! But ... I truly don't want to spend the night talking about the Staton family. Remember, I work at Staton Farms.", Guy protested.

Cassie decided she wouldn't push the topic anymore and would judge the vibe later to see when she could ease in more questions. This was the most she had gathered in her time there and she was sure there was a juicy story behind his comments. So, for the time being, she would sit back and enjoy the ride. The two talked, laughed, and realized that they could bond over their competitive sports history. The more he talked, the more Cassie was captured by his deep warm baritone voice; It was soothing and enveloped her so much that she felt safe in his company. There was no doubt in her mind that she was going to have sex with him that night.

"Well, this is Silverbacks!", Guy announced as he pulled into the parking lot.

It was a full house; it was a definite hot spot for the locals, thought Cassie. When Guy parked, she was about to open the door so she could hop out but she stopped herself. Damn it was hard to allow a man to cater to her, she thought, as she noticed other women waiting for their gentlemen to open their doors. Guy noticed her hesitation and her deliberate decision to wait for him. He thought it would be quite easy for Southern men to pull and snatch every Northern woman away from their men if chivalry wasn't customary there. He realized all he had to do was be himself, a Southern gentleman, and he could easily win her over.

Guy walked around to the passenger side and remembered that she had struggled to get in with her 4-inch heels. Consequently, after opening the door, he extended his strong arm to help steady her so that she could gracefully exit the vehicle. He wanted everyone within sight to see her confidence and sex appeal;

she was nothing like any woman to which that town was accustomed. And Guy was unlike any man Cassie had ever encountered; for the first time that night, she took a good look at her date. Despite being a *cowboy*, as she put it, he wasn't dressed like one, she thought, sure he wore cowboy boots but they were ostrich leather. Nothing about his attire or vehicle suggested farm hand, now that she had seen him during nonworking hours. She was starting to think there was more to him than she first believed and reactions garnered from the patrons spoke volumes as they entered the restaurant.

"Hey Guy!", greeted several men at the pool table.

"Guy!", purred some of the ladies.

Guy was cool and quietly confident with his greetings; to some, he simply nodded while others received a hardy chuckle and hug. To Cassie, it was like witnessing a hometown legend come to visit; everyone wanted a piece of him and to reminisce about old times. Whenever he tried to introduce Cassie, he couldn't get a word in because of a boisterous acquaintance eager to go down memory lane. Trixy, one of the servers, spotted the couple.

"Hey babes, make yourselves comfortable; sit anywhere you like.", shouted Trixy.

Guy led Cassie to a dining table near the pool tables; some patrons had a few games started.

"Aren't you the popular one?", teased Cassie as he assisted her with her chair.

"No, not really; it's just because people don't see me much. I used to hang out a lot, so my friends saw me all the time … but for the last few years all I do is work and if you don't patronize the local shops during work hours then you probably won't see me. The most I do is run business errands, work on the farm, and back home to bed; there's not much time for anything else.", confessed Guy.

"All work and no play, huh? I know a little about that; I've been like that most of my career. I have a few close-knit friends and family who complete my circle, but that's it. I don't make much time for more than that but an occasional guy to make sure my needs are met.", confessed Cassie.

"I guess I'm your Guy for the time being.", flirted Guy.

Cassie laughed then pointed, "Exactly!"

Although those were Cassie's intentions, Guy had much more in mind; he flashed his intoxicating smile and then focused on a much safer topic.

"My circle is small as well, but if my mother had her say it would only be a circle of two, three at the most.", Guy laughed.

"Are you a momma's boy? You must be an only child like me.", teased Cassie.

"Far from it, but I do try to accommodate the old girl; especially since my father died.", Guy explained, "Sometimes Ma acts like I'm the only one, but I have a baby sister named Gal."

"Guy and Gal?", giggled Cassie, "Your parents liked to keep things simple I take it."

"In a way yes.", laughed Guy, "I'm named after my father and grandfather; who knows why they named her Gal. I guess they weren't creative."

The two continued in their laughter as conversation seemed to come easy for them. The only thing that slowed their flow was the waitress.

"Guy, what can I get you and your lady friend?", asked Trixy, the waitress.

"Trixy, I'll take a draft beer. Cassie?", Guy responded.

"I'll take a draft beer too.", Cassie echoed.

"Sounds good. I'll be right back with your drinks. Then you can let me know what else you want. The house special tonight is fried catfish.", informed Trixy.

"Nice! I took you for a wine or light beer type of lady.", chuckled Guy.

"Evidence that you don't know me. I don't like wine.", laughed Cassie, "I'm a brown liquor type of chick and if I'm going to have a beer, I want a real one."

"I like how you roll.", flirted Guy.

"Good because I can only be me and I do me very well.", flirted Cassie, "I am as real as they come, cowboy."

"So, I've met a *real one*?", flirted Guy.

"What do *you* know about a *real one*?', laughed Cassie.

Before Guy could respond their waitress returned with their drinks.

"Here you go, Guy, you've got the ladies jealous and stirred up by bringing your date.", laughed Trixy, "Be careful darling, these women can be real hell cats when they're jealous."

Trixy patted Cassie on the shoulder as she provided the warning.

"Honey, please, they don't want any of this. They will learn fast that I am not one to be fucked with.", smirked Cassie.

"Ok, girlie, I heard that!", laughed Trixy, "The men of your family really know how to pick 'em!"

"He's just showing me around. It's nothing like that.", Cassie informed.

"Okay if you say so, darling.", chuckled Trixy, "I'll be back later to check on you two."

Trixy walked away as she chuckled at Cassie; it was quite plain to see that the two had chemistry and a strong attraction. It was written all over them, thought Trixy.

"So, it's safe to assume your mother isn't one to be fucked with either.", laughed Cassie.

"For damn sure!", laughed Guy, "And one not to let things go. She's determined to see me settle down among other things."

"My auntie is relentless with the same topic. She keeps telling me that work alone is not enough... maybe she's right ...", sighed Cassie.

"I agree with them ... your auntie and my mother, but I'm not going to rush into anything.", Guy challenged, "I want what my parents had and that doesn't come easily."

"Exactly, same here. My parents have a great relationship. Besides, I don't believe in letting people bully me into making a decision. If I'm doing something, you can be assured it's my own damn choice!", Cassie defended.

"Agreed!", insisted Guy.

"Okay!", giggled Cassie and raised her glass for a toast.

Guy beamed at her laughter; it wasn't pretentious trying to be dainty or ultra-feminine, but bold, confident, and sometimes even loud. He toasted his glass with Cassie and hoped it would be the first of many to come.

"Feeling competitive?", questioned Cassie.

"I'm up for a challenge. What do you have in mind?", asked Guy.

"A quick game of pool.", suggested Cassie.

"I'm down. You can choose the game.", suggested Guy.

He flashed his smile while she contemplated her choices.

"What about One Pocket? You know that one?", suggested Cassie.

"Sure do, that sounds good. Trixy, can you give us another round?", shouted Guy.

"Guy, I want some of that catfish too!", Cassie announced.

"Trixy, and a double order of the catfish platter!", shouted Guy.

His voice boomed over the music, televised sports games, and the laughter of the patrons. Trixy nodded as she began to write their order on a slip then began making their drinks as the couple walked over to the pool table. Cassie stretched her arms in front of her as she prepared for the challenge.

"I hope you don't have one of those sensitive male egos. Cause if you do it's going to be crushed tonight.", boasted Cassie.

"A trash talker … I should have known. But just as much as you are a *real one*, I'm a tough one. Don't be fooled by my smile.", warned Guy as he sipped the last dregs of his beer and then racked the balls.

She knew that smile was lethal to any heterosexual female who had an eye for tall muscular Adonis.

"Not just a cowboy, but a tough one to boot.", teased Cassie as she looked at his fancy boots, "I don't know … those boots say differently. You might be more focused on me stepping on your toes and showing the townspeople you're not as awesome as they think."

Guy nodded to acknowledge her skill at trash-talking, but he had a little in him as well. Before he trash-talked, he decided to flex a little, and when he did that, his short sleeve strained to contain his bicep. With each passing second it looked like his shirt would lose and his bi-cep would rip through his sleeve. Cassie couldn't hear the words that were playfully flowing from Guy's lips, all she could see was his body and her mind raced with thoughts of what she would do to it that night.

"Ready?", asked Guy.

"Oh, most definitely, cowboy.", teased Cassie.

For more than you know, Cassie thought as she moved between the pool table and Guy; she then bent forward so that her juicy rear pushed against his masculinity. Guy was frozen in desire and arousal as he felt his penis strain against his already snug jeans. It took every ounce of concentration and determination for him to remember he was in public and was just getting to know Cassie because everything in him wanted to grab and squeeze those hard nipples that had been taunting him all night long!

"Your drinks!", announced Trixy as she set them on the small circular table near their pool table. "Your platters will be up soon."

Trixy's voice brought Guy to his senses and freed him from his trance as the pool balls clanked with Cassie's successful shot. Guy walked over to get a sip of his beer.

"Nothing like that, huh?", whispered Trixy repeating Cassie's statement, "It's good to see you take a break from work and; more importantly, dating again."

Guy blushed and flashed his dazzling smile; he had no idea that it was that obvious that he was into her.

"It's that obvious? Bro, I thought I was more low-key than that.", Guy laughed.

"Not at all. It's easy to see that you both are into each other. Otherwise, I would be asking her out.", teased Trixy.

Guy laughed along with his old friend from high school; they always seemed to have the same taste in women. They even argued over one; however, his male buddies stood clear of anyone he was interested in, but not Trixy. She was more like him than the rest; whatever she wanted she went after. Trixy pointed to another server bringing the food and excused herself to attend to other customers.

"Looks like it's your turn. I thought I was going to have a lucky streak, but I think the smell of the catfish threw me off.", joked Cassie.

Another server placed the platters on the table. The delicious aroma dominated the space.

"Excuses ... excuses.", teased Guy as he grabbed a meaty piece of the steaming hot catfish.

"No fries. What are these?", Cassie pointed to the side dish.

"Fried pickles. Try them, they are incredible!", informed Guy.

Cassie had never even heard of fried pickles; they were battered and smelled good, but she was doubtful about the taste. She hesitantly picked up a few and smelled them before throwing them in her mouth for a quick chew. Her frown quickly changed to a smile.

"So, what do you think?", asked Guy.

"They're good! Almost as good as my pool game is going to be.", laughed Cassie, "Let me see what you can do."

She picked up a few more and looked at them as if she had discovered the eighth wonder of the world. Guy grabbed his favorite stick and reluctantly eyed the balls for a shot; he could have stood there and watched her amazement at fried pickles. He decided he'd better focus and play his best game because she would be furious if she thought he *let* her win. Cassie was so focused on

56

the pickles and fish, that she didn't realize that he hadn't missed yet.

"Sorry, here I come.", Cassie apologized.

"Come for what? It's still my turn.", laughed Guy.

"What?", whispered Cassie.

No way; she hadn't been beaten in years. If he won, she would hear about this every time they saw each other. Finally, his streak ended.

"Damn, Guy!", laughed Cassie, "I thought it was going to be a complete blowout. You finally missed one."

Cassie sighed as she contemplated her next shot, but there was no way for a recovery. The most she could do was have a respectable finish. She missed her first shot.

"Damn! That's too bad.", teased Guy, "Maybe you'll have better luck the next time we play."

"Don't get used to beating me. That was a pure fluke. There were too many distractions and noise.", laughed Cassie.

Guy picked up the book-shaped check presenter to place his credit card inside when Cassie snatched it away.

"I got it.", informed Cassie.

"You don't have to do that.", insisted Guy.

"No worries.", Cassie dismissed.

Cassie flagged Trixy and provided her credit card for payment. Trixy was extremely confused by the gesture; so, she looked at Guy for an explanation.

"Are you serious?", Trixy laughed.

Trixy expected Guy to stop her and give her his card but instead, he shrugged his shoulders.

"She insists.", chuckled Guy.

Guy continued to chuckle at Cassie's assertiveness as the two left the restaurant. Cassie didn't know how much Guy earned, but she didn't feel right about him paying. Especially, considering it was a date of convenience, one of espionage. Besides, Cassie was used to being what was called a boss bitch and that meant she paid her way and most times for the man too. Furthermore, she bested any man she ever dated in everything. Guy was the first who seemed equipped to possibly hold his own, but she reminded herself they were not dating. She was only using him for information and sex; so far that night, she had achieved neither. Perhaps after sleeping with him that night, she would have better luck at the former, she thought as he drove her back home.

"So, what do you think of Silverbacks now?", inquired Guy.

"It was fun. Nothing like I expected, though. It felt like ...", she paused; she wanted to say like home but opted for another phrase, "a cool place to hang out."

"Good. I like it there too. The folks- the staff and customers make everyone feel welcomed.", Guy concurred.

"And that catfish was perfect ...", whispered Cassie, "It's just as good as my Granny's."

Guy laughed at her childlike whisper as if her granny could hear her from hundreds of miles away.

"I promise I'll keep that secret.", chuckled Guy.

"You better! Oh man, it was like there were a bunch of aunties and uncles back there cooking.", laughed Cassie.

"Well, the cooks are aunties and uncles ...", laughed Guy.

Going back, they decided not to play any music and focus on each other. The night air was cooler so, they rode with the windows down as they went along the back roads. Cassie could hear the once unfamiliar sounds that she had come accustomed to, during her stay and the smell of the wild growth was comforting. The ride back was much quicker as those rides often feel. Guy hated for the night to end, but he felt confident that there would be other nights just like that one.

Cassie waited for Guy as she was learning to do; this time it felt natural to wait for his assistance. Guy smiled when he noticed that she patiently waited for him. He opened the door and assisted her down; he decided to plant a gentle kiss on her hand. As odd as it might seem to some to hear, she had never had a man kiss her on her hand. It felt corny to her but thrilling at the same time; like going on a date for the first time in life.

"I'm so glad you agreed to go out with me.", confessed Guy.

He decided he would walk her to the door so that their time together would last a little longer. He slipped his arm around her waist as they walked side by side.

"Me too, cowboy. You surprised me the *whole* night.", flirted Cassie as she looked up at him.

In true Guy fashion, he flashed that smile that had been taking the breath out of her lungs all night. She had a plan that would do the same for his fine ass, she thought, as they reached the front door and stood under the porch light. She entered the code and opened the door.

"If you're free, we can do this again this weekend. I'll call you.", Guy uttered.

He paused when he noticed that look of expectation and yearning in her eyes. He was going to lean down for a polite goodnight kiss when Cassie reached up and pulled his lips to hers. That was a moment his mind had fantasized about all night long.

Just as Cassie was unaccustomed to certain things by the opposite sex, the same was true for Guy. He was normally the aggressor and his past girlfriends often pretended that they didn't want sex as much as he did. It was strangely freeing to know that Cassie matched his passion. The two hungered for the taste of the other as their tongues explored their mouths; then Guy's tongue ventured on another voyage to Cassie's neck. Its flickering motion sent shivers through her body and she pulled him ever closer causing him to feel her hard nipples pressing into his chest.

At that moment he moaned and he looked down to see that they had escaped their knitted confines. He began to reach for them so that he could pull them as he had wanted to all night when she pushed his arms away and pulled his shirt from his pants. She began unbuttoning his shirt; there was no doubt in his mind that she had specific nightcap plans. Plans with which he wasn't comfortable. He wanted more than a one-night stand or a hook-up; a woman as intelligent and accomplished deserved more than that and he was just the *guy* to give it to her.

"Cassie, we should call it a night. I'll call you. I know another great place to take you, a fancier place. You can dress up and stun us all and you don't even need to bring your wallet.", chuckled Guy.

Guy inhaled deeply as he turned away; it was a tough call, but he felt it was the right one to make. Cassie, on the other hand, was disappointed that she didn't have any sexual release. However, she was eager to see him that weekend, and the excitement created by their date would not be in vain. Not only would she use the mojo created by their date to gain information; information that she would use to twist the arms of Bitch Staton to get what she wanted, but she would also have Guy in her bed that weekend.

Chapter 5

Pink arrived at the community center early. She wanted to take control of their meeting and one way she thought of was being there to greet Cassie upon her arrival. Pink had stopped dressing up for the office long ago unless there was an extraordinary person to impress or she wanted to acquire a deal, but she would make an exception for Cassie. Pink didn't want the city slicker to think that she didn't know how to be professional or stylish. Pink wasn't one for dresses, she always felt that her six-foot-frame could overpower a dress. Her muscled arms and legs seemed to command attention even when it was unwanted. She never wore dresses unless she was trying to look sexy or feminine; otherwise, a pantsuit was the perfect attire to represent her strength and position.

Pink selected a monochromatic look of all black; she wore a pair of high-rise flare-legged pants, a mock neck sweater shell, and a blazer. She wore oversized genuine pearl stud earrings with a matching long double-strand pearl necklace and three-inch heeled black and white oxford pumps. Pink sat inside the conference room facing the entrance with her legs crossed and arms folded.

Cassie pulled into the parking lot early so that she could await her foe; at least that was the plan. She parked her vehicle next to a Rolls Royce Ghost in black that she assumed had to belong to Pink Staton.

"Damn! I wanted to get here first.", swore Cassie.

Who else would be there in such luxury and show off their power, but Ms. Staton, thought Cassie. It was at times like this that she was thankful that she had an expansive wardrobe that could compete with the elites. So, they couldn't look down their snobby noses at her, she thought. She wore a high-waisted tan leather pair of flare-legged pants with a front uncentered zipper that flowed down just below the hip line. The pants came with a matching wide-buckled leather belt with a sash that hung down the opposite side of the zipper. It was quite a unique find that Cassie was not able to resist when she eyed it in a boutique. She paired it with a simple cream stretchy mock neck with long sleeves along with her shoes and designer purse from her date with Guy. Unlike last night, she decided to wear her hair in an updo so that her curls gently cascaded over her forehead and she wore medium-sized gold ball stud earrings.

Guy, she thought, he had been on her mind from the time he picked her up for their date to that very moment. Despite daydreaming about him, she was massively disappointed that he hadn't come inside for sex; she had never been turned down by a man before. However, she wasn't discouraged; she considered it an easy challenge to win as it was obvious that his body and his mind wanted her. The pool table incident was a clear indicator of that. Although the date did not end as she expected, she hadn't been able to focus on much of anything but Guy. She had even spent the night and that morning retelling Princess the details of the date with Princess seemingly understanding and loving it all.

"Focus, Cassie. That bitch is inside waiting to devour you if she can.", whispered Cassie as she reached for her briefcase and purse.

She took several deep breaths before she trusted herself to even get out of the car. If this didn't work, she didn't know what would. One thing she knew for certain was that her boss would soon want to escalate her original plan if she didn't make some headway. She just wasn't sure if that was the right way to go about things anymore, now that she had spent time in town and learned a little about the Staton family's reputation.

As Cassie entered the community center, she noticed plaques and pictures on the walls of Staton family members of the past. It was a needed reminder that her foe's family started the town and the town bore her name. Before she could take in more images, she heard someone call her name.

"Ms. Wiliams.", bellowed Henry, the head butler of the Staton household.

"Yes.", Cassie responded hesitantly.

"Right this way. Mrs. Staton is waiting to meet with you.", Henry informed.

Cassie nodded at the mature Black staff member; he was impeccably dressed in a black suit with a black chauffeur hat in hand. She followed him as if Pink Staton had summoned her and she had not been the one to arrange the meeting. She had to think quickly of a way to reclaim the control that Pink had clearly snatched out of her hands. Cassie began to speak as she entered the room.

"Mrs. Staton, thank you for agreeing to meet with me. I'm Ms. Williams.", Cassie boomed as her heels pounded the wooden floor.

Pink stood to greet and shake Cassie's extended hand. She was surprised that Cassie wasn't a petite woman; she had expected that her aggressiveness was a product of one trying to prove that she wasn't fragile in a field dominated by men. Perhaps Cassie was simply like her, born that way.

"Good to place a face with a voice.", Pink provided as she shook Cassie's hand.

Henry smirked as he closed the double doors behind Cassie to provide privacy; he thought it humorous that neither pretended it was nice to meet the other. The ladies were well matched, he thought as he waited outside the room. He could hear Cassie continue talking as she felt she had regained control.

"Yes, agreed. Please have a seat as I know your time is valuable.", Cassie suggested as she sat down, "I'll get straight to the point."

"Please do.", Pink replied as she eyed her watch.

"Staton Holdings Inc. has a few divisions that are dead weight. The biggest one is your newest one, Staton's Pride."

"You have faulty information. Staton's Pride as a division is new, but not as a product or infrastructure. We've expanded our animal feed line to include domesticated animal food products. Thus, Staton's pride was birthed.", chuckled Pink.

"Oh, I'm quite aware of the history, that's why I said what I said.", Cassie spat, "As you just confirmed it was *born* recently. It's dead weight so let us make an offer for it."

"Oh no. My son, uh ...", Pink cleared her throat, "KC, will not agree to that. Staton's Pride is his baby and legacy that he added to our empire."

"Mrs. Staton ... you are making this more difficult than it has to be.", sighed Cassie.

"So, you think that you can chip away at our holdings? Is that your plan? You aren't smarter than me, Ms. Williams. Again, we are not desperate to sell nor are we hard-up for cash. I'm starting to think your boss doesn't like you. Maybe he sent you here as a setup to fail.", Pink declared.

"Mrs. Staton, I am the highest-grossing acquisition closer at my company. That's why they sent me. Don't bother trying to play mind games with me, Mrs. Staton; I am much too smart for that!", sneered Cassie, "Just keep in mind, my company always gets what it wants. The question is, will that acquisition be a win-win for everyone or be a win-lose for you."

"Ms. Williams, as I thought, this was a *complete* waste of time. You must be accustomed to dealing with easily intimidated folks. We have been able to ensure over a hundred years of prosperity because of hard work and determination. So, we don't take well to threats.", bellowed Pink.

Her voice belied the beauty that sat before Cassie; it carried power, strength, and intimidation. However, Cassie was not easily dismissed nor did she like taking no for an answer. She was determined to show up Pink by whatever means were necessary.

"Ms. Williams, there's no need for you to contact me again.", Pink exclaimed.

"Mrs. Staton, this is just the first of future encounters.", declared Cassie.

Pink looked at her sideways and then removed her purse from the table so she could leave. Pink began her exit, but Cassie would not allow Pink to leave the room first. Cassie stormed past Pink with her purse and briefcase in tow; her briefcase clipped Pink's elbow causing her to stop in her tracks. As Cassie exited, her steps echoed throughout the building. In her haste, she passed the one picture of KC Staton III on the wall of the community hall. She missed the one shot she felt was the missing piece of the puzzle; she was willing to bet money that she would have better luck with the son than his tight-lipped, stick-up-her-ass momma.

Pink stood in place; she was shocked by the arrogance of the northerner. She was so thankful that from the looks of things, her son had not contacted Ms. Williams as she had previously feared. So now, she thought, she had to figure out what on earth he could have been talking about yesterday; what would change the family forever?

"Henry, let's give the little bitch time to get in her car and leave before you take me home. I don't want to have any more words with her.", chuckled Pink, "Because if she says the wrong thing to me right now ... *right* now!"

"Agreed ma'am.", nodded Henry.

Henry had known her since they were teens and had seen her get into lots of scuffles with girls and boys; none was left standing after a round with her. She even kicked her husband's ass when they were teens because out of his shyness, he had said the wrong thing. The poor thing thought Henry, KC Jr. was just trying to get a date.

"Ok, bitch!", mumbled Cassie as she entered her car, "You want to see my ugly side, bitch?"

Cassie sped from the parking lot and had to regain her composure; the last thing she needed was to be pulled over by the police who were literally in Pink's pocket. That would be so humiliating, sighed Cassie as she took deep breaths to calm down and slow her speed.

"Guy, this is why I need a good fuck!", shouted Cassie.

Cassie drove the familiar route to the shops downtown and decided to stop by Jill's boutique and check on her order. She could use a good distraction and from the looks of things that's all she could depend on at that point. She was sure that the items should be there despite not receiving a call from Jill; if they were there, she'd take them straight to the post office and package them individually to her mother, aunt, and grandmother. Just then, she noticed Guy carrying a box toward Jill's shop.

"Just who I need to see!", Cassie rejoiced.

So, she turned on a dime and hit the curb as she made a sharp right turn into the parking lot.

"Shit! Don't fuck up your rental.", Cassie reprimanded herself.

She began to giggle, but it quickly turned into laughter as she remembered that she once accused him of stalking her and now she was excited to see him.

"Now *I'm* stalking *his ass*.", laughed Cassie.

66

Cassie unpinned her hair and ran her fingers through it. She knew Guy loved her hair and there was a gentle breeze that would cause her curls to dance. She was eager to get his attention because she was fiending for him and also for a way to release her anger and frustration. She didn't even want to think about the call she would have to make to her boss later that day. She was dreading it. Cassie almost jogged to catch up with Guy before he dropped off his package and left to go who knows where. She entered the boutique breathing heavily and hoping that it would go unnoticed.

"Hi, Cassie! You are just in time. Guy dropped off your order.", announced Jill.

"Hey, Jill, that's awesome and perfect timing. I came to check on it.", blurted Cassie then her eyes became fixated on Guy and her voice changed to a deeper whisper, "Guy, good to see you again."

She hoped the two would assume she was being seductive rather than out of breath as she approached the counter clearing her throat.

"Hey, Cassie!", beamed Guy.

He quickly approached her for a hug; it was one of those hugs you give when you haven't seen someone you love in a long time. It felt so good to Cassie; she couldn't help but lean into it as she wrapped her arms possessively around his waist. Jill blushed as their body language said they were ready for things that should not be done in public.

"Well Cassie, I see a whole lot has changed since you were here last.", giggled Jill.

"A little.", teased Guy, and then he kissed Cassie on the forehead.

Cassie giggled and then blushed; she was instantly embarrassed that she was acting like an inexperienced girl, but there was something about Guy that could do that to a woman. Jill giggled too and reached over and playfully tapped Cassie on the hand.

"Girl, it seems your timing is on point; not just to get your order, but for Guy too!", giggled Jill, "His mother, Ms. Rose, finished your order pretty fast."

"What? Guy, why didn't you tell me your mother was the artist?", questioned Cassie.

Jill threw Guy an apologetic look and then walked to the storage room to pretend that she was looking for something.

"Well, it didn't seem important at the time. Besides, I had no idea I would be lucky enough to get you out on a date.", laughed Guy.

"The way you were stalking me, I think you knew.", laughed Cassie.

"I was not. I was just doing my regular routine; you were the newbie in town stalking me.", Guy chuckled.

"You wish.", laughed Cassie as she poked his rock-hard abdomen.

Cassie removed a figurine from the box on the counter and gazed at it.

"I'm still in shock. Your mother's art is so detailed and gorgeous! I pictured a little old lady with a magnifying glass working on every detail.", giggled Cassie as she set it gently back in the box.

"Not my mother; far from it.", Guy roared with laughter.

He noticed a stray curl resting on her face and he couldn't control the urge to touch it and place it behind her ear; so, he did just that and kissed her on the cheek.

"I've been thinking about you since last night…", Guy whispered.

He was about to admit that he regretted his decision to leave when Cassie interrupted him.

"Maybe we could have dinner together tonight?", she suggested.

"That sounds good. I can prepare a little something for us … at my place. You can follow me there or ride with me.", he suggested.

"That's a great idea, but I just need to check on Princess first. She has been alone most of the day.", Cassie explained.

"Okay, but you can bring her with you if you want. Boy and I would love to see her.", Guy chuckled.

"Oh, I just remembered I was going to swing by the post office and mail the figurines if they were here.", sighed Cassie.

Jill joined the pair flashing the broadest smile.

"Don't worry about that. If you want you can text me the addresses you want them sent to and I can handle it. You can pay for the postage and figurines after I mail them.", suggested Jill with a wink at Guy.

Cassie could see that Jill was on team Gussie (an ugly couple shipping name) and Jill was willing to do whatever she could to help his plans. Cassie appreciated it but she wanted more than a meal unless it included what Guy was packing.

"Thanks, Jill, I appreciate that!", Cassie cheered.

"So, Cassie, I'll text you the address to my cabin and I'll head there to get the meal started.", announced Guy as he started walking backward toward the door.

Jill smiled at Cassie whose eyes followed Guy's every movement as he turned around to exit. Jill was quite aware of that look; all his ex-girlfriends often had it; it was a look that said they wanted to devour him. Jill had known Guy long enough to see that he felt something special for Cassie. She hoped that Cassie wasn't like the mean bitches he seemed to be attracted to, that seemed to always move on, but never before they crushed his heart.

"Earth to Cassie.", teased Jill.

"Oh ...", laughed Cassie.

"I don't mean to butt in your business ...", Jill began.

"So, don't ...", Cassie laughed.

"Guy is a great man and a friend. Please don't hurt him ...", Jill confided.

"I have absolutely no intentions of that. Trust me, Guy knows what time it is. He's a grown-ass man.", Cassie informed.

Jill nodded but really didn't know what Cassie meant by that, but she would leave the topic alone after all Cassie and Guy were just that, two grown-ass people who could handle the chips as they fell. She just hoped that the chips would not come crashing down atop Guy's head.

"Talk later. I'll send the addresses in a bit.", Cassie informed.

"Okay, no rush.", assured Jill.

Cassie couldn't exit the store fast enough. She was more eager than she had ever been to have sex with a man. She convinced herself it was the stress and the desperate need to relieve it. However, there was a nagging thought that it was something different; yet it was not the time to even entertain such thoughts. She had too much on the line and a cowboy was not worth risking everything. Just then her cell rang with a much too familiar ringtone; it was her boss, Kenneth Fitzpatrick.

"Fitzpatrick.", greeted Cassie.

"Cassie, you are past due for an update. This isn't like you. I'm almost afraid to get one.", Kenneth advised.

"Fitz, this one is a challenge and I'm thinking I might need to take a leave to give myself time to thoroughly think this through...", Cassie explained.

"Think things through? You've already done that; you discussed a contingency plan that would surely seal the deal. You just need to put it in play.", Kenneth reminded.

"That was more bravado than an actual plan. Besides, I don't want to do that...", Cassie confessed.

"Bravado or not; it was genius nevertheless!", Kenneth began, "Take the time you need, but if it's too long, I'll have to bring in a backup."

"Agreed.", Cassie provided before disconnecting the call.

The old Cassie would not have hesitated and would have enacted the plan and not even met with Pink Staton that day. But Cassie found something heartwarming about the town of Staton and the surrounding area that made her look at things differently. She was never more aware of it than when she went into town and watched the families walking down the main street. Family meant everything to the people of Staton; it was even starting to tug at her heartstrings. God knows she thought, how closed off her heart had been to family and marriage; it was nothing that ever concerned her. Yet, after seeing the people, their closeness, and commitment, she could envision herself there with a family and a little one in a stroller. Another call interrupted her thoughts as she opened her car door.

"Micki! Hey!", greeted Cassie.

"Girl, I've been waiting for the details about last night and you've gone silent on me.", fussed Michelle.

"Sorry, nothing has gone right since last night … mostly.", sighed Cassie.

Cassie caught Michelle up on her date with Guy and her disastrous meeting with Pink Staton.

"Well, you'll get that dick tonight for sure. But Pink …", sighed Michelle.

"She's a real bitch that won't fold.", Cassie sighed.

"Wow, so you've finally been out bitched!", laughed Michelle, "You might have to get raw and dirty with her."

"Exactly, I might have to put plan B in motion.", Cassie sighed again.

"No! Would you really do that? I assumed you were joking when you told me about that.", fussed Michelle.

"No, I was dead serious, but now …", sighed Cassie, "I truthfully don't want to. I'm going to take some time off from work and clear my head to get a handle on things."

"Are you going soft on me? The old Cassie never changed her mind. Granted, it's okay if you don't do it. You don't have to win at any cost.", Michelle counseled.

"I don't know what's happening to me. I don't even recognize myself anymore. This place has me thinking about things I *never* think about.", whispered Cassie.

"Why are you whispering? Does it have you wanting to kill somebody?", joked Michelle.

"No, something even scarier, like getting married and having a family.", laughed Cassie.

"What? I know you're fucking lying.", shouted Michelle.

"Okay, so you see my point! That's why I need to take a break and get my head back in the game!", retorted Cassie.

"Nothing gets my head right, like a good fuck! Make sure you get that white boy in bed tonight.", laughed Michelle.

"Oh, I plan on it. At this point, I don't care if I have to rape his ass.", laughed Cassie.

"I feel you!", attested Michelle.

The two hollered and laughed at the thought of Cassie manhandling Guy's six-foot-four frame and having her way with him.

"Speaking of men ... have you found a new boyfriend yet?", questioned Cassie.

"Girl, please. I've decided I'm only taking candidates for fucking. Anything else is too hard to find.", laughed Michelle.

Michelle talked a tough game, but she was venturing into a soft girl era just like Cassie and wanted more as well. Cassie and Michelle had been women for whom *more* had never been enough.

"It's hard for a successful black woman to find suitable options.", Cassie concurred.

"But you got lucky.", laughed Michelle, "I'm going to let you go. I don't want to slow you down not one bit. Go get sexy and snag that dick! Bye."

"Okay ... bye", giggled Cassie and then she disconnected.

Guy arrived at the cabin at the speed of the gods.

"Boy!", shouted Guy.

Boy came running from his water bowl.

"We are having guests, Cassie and Princess are coming.", beamed Guy as Boy howled his approval.

Guy was thankful that Cassie wasn't an elitist when it came to food and she enjoyed some of the same dishes a single man enjoys. Consequently, he had everything on hand to prepare a quick and decent meal for her. He pulled the catfish from the fridge that he had thawing, his homemade seasoning mix, and cornmeal. He even had pickles that he could batter and deep fry since she had just discovered their delicious flavor. He hoped a casual and private atmosphere would be what they needed to fully open up and he was willing to allow her to open herself up completely to him that night. He would not shut her advances down; she could have all of him, he smirked at the thought.

"Princess! Come here, girl! We have a date!", shouted Cassie as she entered the rental house.

Princess came bolting from the bedroom with excitement as if she knew just what the night had in store for her owner. She jumped up and rested her front paws on Cassie as she wagged her tail.

"Guy invited us over for dinner. Down girl; I need to freshen up and change clothes.", giggled Cassie.

Cassie pranced to the bedroom to quickly look through her outfits. The Southern Spring weather was much warmer than she had back home, so she hadn't realized that she could have brought some shorts. The only pair she had was a pair that she lounged in, but she would wear them anyway. They were cut-off blue jeans that were extremely short and revealed her butt cheeks and the inner pocket flaps. She pulled out her white plunging neck cropped backless halter to wear with it. She slipped on a pair of taupe plaid stiletto mules.

"Woof! Woof!", Princess barked behind her owner.

"Wait, girl! I need to freshen up, then we'll be ready to leave.", laughed Cassie.

Guy was pleased that everything was smelling good. He had even set a small flower arrangement on the dining room table. He often picked flowers from his garden and brought them inside; it always reminded him of his grandmother, who felt that flowers made a house feel like a home. He figured that Cassie should be arriving any minute and when she did, he wanted the food to be piping hot for her.

"Okay, girl let's go.", instructed Cassie.

However, before she left, she eyed two of Princess' leashes. She quickly grabbed them and headed out to the car with Princess taking the lead. As she drove the route, GPS indicated that his home was near. She was surprised at how close he lived to her rental home, but she shouldn't have been surprised because of how they met. It would be nice to get a glimpse of his world; was he a neat freak or was he messy? These were thoughts running through her mind. She truly hoped his bedroom was clean; otherwise, that would mess up the vibe and the plans she had for him.

Cassie slowly pulled into his drive. She was surprised to see such an adorable cabin; flowers were growing around it. It was picture-perfect; it was a single-story wood frame cabin that was painted grey. There was a huge cobblestone fireplace in the front and a side deck. She was surprised to see that the gorgeous flowers were planted with such care and detail not just around the cabin but throughout the property. It was nothing at all like what she expected the cowboy to call home. She was starting to see there was so much more to him than what she saw on the surface.

After exiting the vehicle, she opened the rear passenger door and Princess darted toward the cabin as if she had been there a thousand times while barking every step of the way. Guy heard Princess announce their arrival and opened the door to greet them with the broadest smile. Cassie was finally open to seeing a glimpse of Guy's true vibe; he had a country gentleman feel to him.

"Welcome, ladies!", Guy's voice boomed as he patted Princess and rubbed her ears.

"Hey, Cowboy! I was not expecting this!", laughed Cassie as she approached the entrance with the leashes in hand.

"You haven't seen anything yet!", laughed Guy.

Their laughter stopped when he possessively pulled her close and kissed her as if he hadn't seen her in months. That kiss was even more intoxicating than their first and promised to be just the first of the many pleasures that were yet to come. Guy regained his composure before his manhood appeared, but it was desperate to make its presence known. Cassie felt shivers coarse through her body as her desire grew and she began to think of what she would do to the cowboy once inside.

"Come on in and make yourself at home.", welcomed Guy.

Guy allowed his eyes to follow Cassie's movements as she entered the neat and cozy cabin to find Princess and Boy playing like long-lost brother and sister. He almost left his door open when he noticed her full butt cheeks playing peekaboo with her shorts. Cassie hung her purse and the leashes on the rack just inside the entrance on the wall. Her eyes scanned the interior to see the cobblestone fireplace sore to the ceiling. There were decorative pieces on the mantel that looked hand-crafted, perhaps by his mother. She picked up one piece to examine it more closely.

"My maternal grandmother, Caroline, made that years ago. She was very creative, an artist, I guess one could say. My mother inherited those skills, but that's where it ends. My sister, Gal, and I have absolutely no artistic abilities at all.", laughed Guy.

Cassie walked around the spacious great room; it was built in an open concept before an open concept was even a thing. She eyed some of the paintings mounted on the wall. She touched the canvas and traced her fingers along the delicate lines of the adorable blond boy depicted.

"Yes, that's me when I was about ten. My granny Caroline painted it.", Guy provided as he responded to the question her eyes revealed, "I probably should tell you ..."

Cassie could see the seriousness in his eyes as if he were going to confess feelings or ask her to be his girlfriend. She felt he had already told her too much when he gave a history lesson about his family. She wasn't ready for all that or even sure if she wanted anything from the small town more than a good time and a profitable business deal.

"Cowboy, let's keep things light and fun.", Cassie insisted.

Guy nodded his agreement and returned to the kitchen area on the other side of the cabin to wash his hands as if he was never about to confess anything. Then he continued setting the table while Cassie walked around the space and touched other trinkets and his sofa as if they were magically speaking to her and telling her the secrets of the man who had captured her mind and aroused her body. She touched the soft, yet worn oversized brown leather tufted sectional sofa that faced the fireplace. There was an old throw tossed over the back that she thought might also have been handmade. She noticed a few books on the coffee table, an ashtray with a partially smoked cigar, and an antique wooden box that might have contained more cigars.

"Well dinner is ready.", announced Guy, "You can freshen up in the kitchen sink".

He placed a serving platter of golden fried catfish and pickles on the kitchen dining table. Afterward, he pulled another feeding bowl from a cabinet, grabbed a package of Staton's Pride from the refrigerator, and poured it into the dog bowls.

"Can't leave you two out.", chuckled Guy as the two dogs came running.

Cassie walked to the dining table; she had never been somewhere, where at every turn there was an antique or something old that seemed to have a story. She wondered about the stories the table could tell as she viewed the meal displayed.

"This looks so good. I thought I smelled catfish.", beamed Cassie, "Who delivered it?"

"What? Cowboys do have skills.", joked Guy, "Would you like a beer?"

"Yeah, that sounds good.", said Cassie.

She sat at the table and placed a couple of catfish fillets on her plate. Afterward, she scooped a tong full of fried pickles placing them next to the fish. She couldn't wait to dig in; the fish looked delicious and perfectly fried. She hoped looks were not deceiving; her eyes locked with his as she took a bite. Guy laughed as her eyes and face revealed that she loved it.

"See, ah ha. You thought I didn't know what I was doing.", laughed Guy.

"I taste seasoning!", gasped Cassie, "You white folks usually don't use it."

"Maybe that's how Northern white folks do it, but all Southerners know how to cook!", chuckled Guy.

Cassie giggled at his response and was glad that they were comfortable enough to speak openly. Guy continued laughing as he handed her a bottle of beer and then sat across from her. He smiled as he fixed his plate; he was pleased to see how much she was enjoying the meal. When he finished fixing it, she playfully took a piece of fish from his plate and tossed it on hers.

"You are one of those dudes that a chick has a hard time figuring out.", laughed Cassie as she marveled at the delicious food.

"Not really if a lady is open-minded and not accusing me of being a stalker.", Guy paused with a smirk.

"Okay, so you're also a comedian too.", laughed Cassie, "I can admit I used stereotypes to box you in. I can admit to being wrong."

"Good, because there is so much more of me, I'd like to share.", whispered Guy.

Cassie knew what she was ready for him to share and it did not involve words. She slipped off her heels and began to explore his legs with her feet. As she sipped her beer, she allowed her feet to explore even greater depths until they reached the hardest piece of wood at the table. Guy had been fighting to control his desire for Cassie, but with the touch of her slender feet he was ready to explode and he was done with denying himself and her. He rose to his feet and without any indication he lifted Cassie and carried her to his bedroom. When he placed her on her feet, she started pulling his shirt from his jeans and accidentally ripped the buttons. A hint of his deep V-shape cut in his abs peeked above the waistline of his jeans and it aroused her immensely causing her to frantically unzip his jeans.

Guy might have carried her to the bedroom, but Cassie was the one in charge then. She pulled his body close to hers as she kissed him and explored his mouth with her tongue. When his tongue began to dominate, she puckered her lips and pushed and pulled his head in and out to simulate the thrust of his penis and it was a preshow of what was forthcoming. Guy moaned; he had never experienced a woman doing that. He realized then that Cassie was quite knowledgeable and he was all too willing to be her student if necessary. Cassie began a strip tease as she removed her skimpy clothing to reveal her full breasts and huge nipples. Guy almost tripped while disrobing because his gaze and desire were fixated on them.

"Let's walk", shouted Cassie.

Princess heard the command and then grabbed the leashes from the rack. Guy was confused by the statement and had even more questions about it when Princess rushed inside the bedroom with the leashes.

"Good girl. Now go.", ordered Cassie.

Guy continued to look confused until Cassie pushed him onto the bed and jumped on top of him. She skillfully tied his hands to the iron headboard and then smirked at Guy with a hint of the siren within. Guy knew that loving her could be dangerous if she didn't return those feelings; a man could become obsessed with her. She removed the rubber band that supported his man bun and then massaged his scalp before she ran her fingernails over it. With each touch, she would provide pleasure and then deliver a little pain afterward. She explored his muscled chest with her lips, then licked his nipples and when she heard him breathe deeply, she pulled them with her teeth. She searched his chest with her hands down to his pelvis and then started from the top again, but this time using her fingernails to dig deep as she explored. Guy couldn't believe what he was experiencing, he had never allowed a woman that much control despite loving strong-willed and spirited women. Cassie could feel his manhood growing beneath her. She spotted condoms on the nightstand alongside the bed.

"A little sure of yourself, huh?", laughed Cassie as she reached for the packet.

She quickly tore it open, removed the condom, and placed it on his massive penis. She moaned when she slid the condom on. Whoever said all white men have small dicks, never saw his fine white ass, thought Cassie. With her knees bent, she stood on her feet to ease his penis inside, and she moaned as she slid its thickness within her. Once filled, she began to bounce and gyrate her hips trying to get it deeper and deeper still until she felt it pound against her cervix. Her moans became groans then turned to desperate cries for more pleasure.

Princess and Dog stared at the plates of fish and then they looked down the hall after hearing the moans of their masters. Then they stared at each other before scarfing down the fish.

Guy was out of his mind with pleasure and desire and wouldn't be confined anymore. He pulled against the leash and rail once and was freed; then he freed the other arm as Cassie smiled with pleasure and admiration for his power. He flipped her to her back and began thrusting and pounding her until her passionate cries drove him mad. His animalistic nature took control and his breath became heavy causing his body to shake and moan so deep; his moans came forth that sounded like growls. With the power of his last orgasmic thrust, the bed frame collapsed and the two fell from the bed.

"Shit!", moaned Guy.

Guy held her close and flipped them so that they would land on his back. He chuckled as he kissed her forehead, and cheeks before devouring her lips. The dogs came running to check on what had caused the loud noise and then stood at the entryway; Boy began to howl. To Cassie's surprise and amusement, Guy joined Boy with the loudest boyish howl. Guy laughed as Boy and Princess came close to check on them and Cassie snuggled in his arms.

"Boy, your breath smells like fish.", accused Guy.

Princess and Boy ran off as a sign of guilt, but the dogs weren't the only ones who felt guilty.

"Guy, I am so sorry about the bed. Isn't it an antique?", questioned Cassie.

"It is, but don't you worry about that. It's nothing that can't be repaired or replaced.", reassured Guy.

Guy snuggled Cassie and thought of the future he wanted to create with her. Cassie breathed in his masculine scent as she buried her face in his chest; It was the first time she'd ever felt that she was right where she belonged.

Chapter 6

"Mr. Fitzpatrick, you have a call from Raymond, Mississippi.", announced the secretary.

"Who is it?", questioned Fitzpatrick.

He wondered if it was Ms. Staton reaching out to him despite that being a long shot.

"He refuses to provide a name.", she informed.

"Interesting … okay transfer the call.", instructed Fitzpatrick.

"Mr. Fitzpatrick?", inquired the caller.

"Yes, this is he. Sir, how may I help you?', asked Fitzpatrick.

"I hear you are looking to acquire Staton Farms.", the caller reported.

"What if we are?", Fitzpatrick asked.

"Then I can help. I know a sure way to make that bitch, Pink Staton, fold.", the caller provided.

"Just how much are you looking to get?", Fitzpatrick inquired.

"Not a damn thing. I would be doing this to avenge my family.", the caller informed.

"I already have someone assigned – ", Fitzpatrick began.

"Who obviously can't get the job done.", the caller informed.

"You make a good point. I'll entertain a discussion. What are your thoughts?", Fitzpatrick probed.

Cassie was enjoying her leave of absence too much; it had been a few weeks, but it felt much shorter. She had always said taking time off from work was overrated, but she was starting to doubt those old sentiments. She and Guy had been having the best of times dating; they went on sightseeing ventures and dates. They took turns staying the night at each other's places. She even had shown off some of her cooking skills by preparing him breakfast, but she had to confess that was the limit to her cooking expertise. If Cassie could live the rest of her life like that she would. Princess rushed into the bedroom with her leash in hand.

"Girl, I need more rest. Guy has worn me out the last few days.", sighed Cassie.

The last few days had been filled with endless sex and laughter. It was literally picture-perfect; even the dogs played and got along like long-lost siblings. She wondered what he was up to while she lay in the bed reminiscing. She reached for her cell and gave him a call.

"Good morning! How's my sassy Cassie?", beamed Guy.

"Hey Boo, I'm just missing you. I've gotten used to being awakened by your kisses and having morning sex.", Cassie flirted.

"Well, I can easily make part of that come true this morning.", chuckled Guy, "You must have a sixth sense because I was just about to call you."

"I wish I did have magical powers.", laughed Cassie, she would have used them to solve the Pink Staton problem, "So, what's going on?"

"My friend Pete invited his best buds over for food and drinks. I was hoping you would join me.", Guy asked hesitantly.

He knew full well what an invite like that implied and he hoped to God that she wouldn't decline. The old Cassie most definitely would have declined because she never wanted her sex partners to catch feelings and when she noticed that they were, she ended it with the quickness. This softer side of Cassie was relaxed and reveling in the new experience of courting. Before she could respond, Princess barked her greeting and approval to Guy.

"Tell Princess hello.", laughed Guy.

"Princess, did you hear your buddy?", laughed Cassie, "When is the get-together?"

"It's tonight. I hope that's not too last minute.", Guy informed.

"No, that's plenty of time. I can join you.", Cassie confirmed.

"Great! I can pick you up at 6 pm.", Guy suggested.

"Sounds good. See you then, Boo.", Cassie replied.

Cassie and Guy both were stunned when they ended the call. Guy hadn't introduced a girlfriend to his friends in years and Cassie had never wanted to meet friends of anyone she was screwing, but she had to admit to herself that this was more than that. She realized that she was essentially building a relationship.

"Well damn.", whispered Cassie.

Before Cassie could fully allow the realization to sink in, Michelle called. Cassie sighed as she realized she had been so caught up in Guy she hadn't returned any of the missed calls from her best friend.

"Hey, girl. Sorry, I haven't reached back.", Cassie pleaded.

"I was about to catch a flight down there. What the fuck has been going on with you?", Michelle demanded.

"Nothing but Guy.", laughed Cassie.

"I know you're fucking kidding me right now. It sounds like you are in love.", Michelle proclaimed.

"Girl, I don't know what I'm feeling, but I'm loving it!", screeched Cassie.

"What the fuck has this white nigga done to you!", laughed Michelle.

"Where do I start … His dick is big as fuck! His sex is amazing … *he* is amazing!", giggled Cassie, "We even broke an iron bedframe. Iron!"

"Shit! His dick is *big*?", questioned Michelle.

"Girl, yes! The biggest I've ever seen.", laughed Cassie.

"Even bigger than Jaquan?", questioned Michelle.

"Yes! Jaquan can have several seats and take notes!", laughed Cassie, "My body is completely worn out. We've had sex in every room at his cabin and here at my rental."

"Ooh girl! Tell me more.", begged Michelle.

"Well, on that first night, I let my alter ego out.", joked Cassie.

"Ah, shit! You let Cash Money out of the bag?", hollered Michelle.

"Girl, yes! I tied his wrists to the headboard and rode that big dick! And this strong ass nigga, pulled his arm forward and snapped the leash and then untied the other! I was dripping wet!", hollered Cassie.

"Oh shit!", shouted Michelle.

"Girl, when he did that! I said to myself, that motherfucka can have me! Bitch, I was thinking … how do you want it, where do

86

you want it … when do you want it my white nigga!", screeched Cassie.

"I'm happy for you since we both seem to be flowing into a soft-girl era. Who would have ever guessed this would happen? You actually took my advice and got a good fuck!", cheered Michelle.

"Girl, who you tellin'?", laughed Cassie, "Coming down South and then taking this leave of absence has opened my eyes to something new. I even agreed to meet his friends."

"Shut the fuck up!", shouted Michelle, "You honestly are a new Cassie!"

"Girl, that shit just snuck up on me!", laughed Cassie, "But I must admit, it feels nice."

"Wow, the old Cassie would have been talking about losing her Black card if she ever dated a white man.", laughed Michelle.

"It has come across my mind once or twice …", sighed Cassie.

Cassie imagined what her civil rights activist father might have to say about it.

"I can hear your Auntie Gloria saying, 'Would you rather have an *alone* card cause that's what holding onto that Black card will turn into?' And your mother agreeing.", laughed Michelle.

"I know, right!", laughed Cassie, "Well neither my mother nor Auntie has to worry. I think I'm diving in head first!"

"I can't wait to hear more!", giggled Michelle, "And let me know if one of his friends is rich."

"Girl, please. Guy isn't *even* rich!", laughed Cassie, "Well I better get off the phone. I need to walk Princess and then figure out what to wear. I want all his friends envying him when they see me looking fine as fuck."

"I know that's right!", laughed Michelle.

Guy was running down the stairs like an excited kid when Rose spotted him.

"Hey, sweets. Where are you off to this morning? I need you to run some errands.", Rose informed.

Guy replied as he descended the last few stairs to the foyer of the family home.

"Ma, I can't I'm heading Downtown to pick up a gift for my girl.", informed Guy.

"Your girl? I didn't know you were dating.", his mother admitted.

"Yeah, I've kept it quiet because I didn't think I had a real shot at her. She's one in a million. She's a lot like you actually.", Guy confided.

"Oh boy! I don't know if the household can handle two bitches.", laughed Rose, "Well at least tell me her name."

"She's not from around here, so you don't know her. I'll tell you all about her in due time.", Guy uttered quickly as he kissed Rose on the cheek, "I've got to go."

"Don't keep her a secret ...", teased Rose as her son dashed past her, "I want to make a special figurine for her."

"You already have. She placed an order with Jill.", shouted Guy as he exited the front door.

"I guess I'll make another cute figurine to give her when he brings her by the house.", Rose announced to herself as she mentally started planning a menu for that upcoming occasion.

Guy drove into town to pick up the gift he had ordered for Cassie. When he ordered it, he figured it would be a goodbye gift and a reminder to her of what they could have shared. But after the last few weeks, it seemed to be a promise of more to come instead. Guy beamed at the thought of presenting it to Cassie and reading the heartfelt note he planned to attach. Leave it up to Jill to help him come up with the idea, he thought, as he pulled up in front of her store.

"Good morning, Jill!", Guy beamed.

"Yes, it is and it will be an even better evening for you and Cassie.", laughed Jill.

She retrieved the box from beneath the counter and set it on top.

"I am so excited for you!", giggled Jill.

"Excited doesn't even begin to describe it. I feel nervous like I'm proposing or something.", chuckled Guy.

"Well, I'm sure that's coming next!", teased Jill.

Guy inhaled and exhaled deeply as he opened the packaging; he had decided not to use the local jewelry store but to order a custom piece from a designer upstate who was an acquaintance of Jill. Jill gasped as she eyed the delicate perfection and Guy's eyes seemingly filled with tears that he quickly wiped away as he cleared his throat.

"I'm speechless and I hope Cassie will be as well.", Guy whispered.

He quickly but gently placed the item back in the box, chuckled, and then turned to leave.

"Go get her cowboy!", shouted Jill as she used Cassie's nickname for him.

Cassie was shocked at how fast the day had flown by as she stood looking at a few options to wear. She wanted to be sexy, yet still elegant; elegant but not untouchable as if she was above his friends. She kept returning to the burgundy leotard on her bed. It was made with a soft material and had long sleeves with a buttoned cuff. The plunging neckline and gathered waist would show off her best assets; however, the G-string bottom would be great for later when Guy would rip her clothes off. She found a pair of skin-tight dark blue jeans that she could easily pull her 3-inch knee-high patchwork stiletto boots over the leg. The pair of boots had a mock lace-up front with a side zipper. She thought that the patchwork of her boots matched her outfit perfectly; there were shades of blue, yellow, red, and burgundy. Lastly, she pulled a layered gold-tone necklace overhead to lay upon her heaving bosom.

As she readied herself, she had the strangest feeling that Guy had something up his plaid sleeve but she didn't know what. She was slightly nervous at the thought; in the past, she never gave the vibe to men to encourage them to give gifts or make romantic gestures. She had to be honest with herself this was out of her realm and she assumed anything was possible from the cowboy. Princess' footsteps drew Cassie out of her thoughts and when she turned her attention to Princess, she noticed her dog chasing her tail. That caused Cassie's immediate laughter.

"So, you sense something too, huh girl?", laughed Cassie.

The doorbell rang and Princess instantly ran from the room leaving Cassie there fretting as she quickly glanced at her reflection in the mirror.

"Damn, I didn't get a chance to do my hair or put on any earrings.", Cassie fussed and then fluffed her curls as she headed to the door.

Princess sat in front of the door as if she was able to open it. Cassie shooed her away.

"Really, Princess?", fussed Cassie.

Cassie opened the door to find Guy standing with a beautiful bouquet of white roses and a gift box, but she was more fixated on him. He stood dashing with his soft curled blond hair flowing over his taunt-muscled shoulders instead of his bun.   He wore a chestnut brown dress shirt that seemed to hug every muscled inch of his arms and physique appearing that his bi-ceps would rip through the fabric.

Cassie barely noticed the flowers and did not extend her hand to take them. She continued to examine her cowboy's frame. He wore a chestnut Gucci signature belt with a gold rectangular buckle with the name stamped on it. He surely didn't fit the part of a cowboy; she thought as her eyes continued to roam his body down to his thick thighs. The rich deep blue denim boot-cut jeans barely contained anything- not his ass, his thighs, or his dick, thought Cassie. The only thing rugged about the crisp jeans was the western trim on his pockets; everything else was not. The gold stitching on the jeans made his shirt and belt pop even more. Cassie couldn't wait for him to walk past her so she could see his muscled buttocks. She imagined how he would look shirtless in the low-rise jeans. She quickly glanced downward at his feet to see polished chestnut brown squared-toed alligator cowboy boots with a short shaft.

Guy didn't understand why she was not more focused on the beautiful bouquet that he attempted to give her. He had purposefully chosen the white roses to represent the purity and loyalty of his love for her with which he had hoped to impress her. Little did he realize, she was impressed; however, it was by another package he presented at her doorstep.

"Hello, beautiful.", Guy greeted Cassie with the sweetest kiss on her forehead and then greeted the dog, "I can't forget about my Princess".

Cassie took the items from Guy freeing his hands so that he could show some affection to Princess who enjoyed attention just as much as her owner. Cassie inhaled the scent and beauty of the bouquet; never had she received one as massive. She laid it gently on the countertop. It had to be at least two dozen, she assumed as she hesitantly opened the beautiful gift box. She supposed it couldn't be a ring since they hadn't been dating long enough for an engagement; although her grandmother had only known her grandfather a week before he proposed.

Guy smirked as he watched her nervously hold and then open the gift box; he guessed at the thoughts running through her mind. She opened the box and nearly dropped it as she gasped at the expensive piece. It was a pendant made of white mother of pearl shaped like the Magnolia flower with a large yellow diamond as the pistol and one lone green leaf made from emeralds on a 14-karat gold wheat style chain. If not for the material description on a note by the artisan, she would have assumed it was fake.

"Guy ... how can you?", questioned Cassie.

She did not finish her question as she realized it was rude to ask a man how he could afford such a piece, but she had said enough that Guy understood what she was asking.

"Remember beautiful, I told you that you never have to open your purse again when we are together.", Guy reminded, "So the only question of the hour, should be me asking you if you like it."

"Cowboy, who wouldn't like it? It's gorgeous.", giggled Cassie as she held it by the chain.

"Here, let me put it on.", Guy informed as he took the delicate flower.

Cassie removed her other necklace; next, she swooped her hair up out of the way as Guy placed his gift on her neck. The delicate piece sat atop her cleavage. Guy inhaled deeply as he made sure the pendant sat right side up; he allowed his fingers to linger for a bit as he thought about what he would do to her breasts later that night.

"There's one more part to your gift.", Guy stated.

Cassie excitedly looked at the box and then at the roses; it was there that she found a gold envelope.

"May I?", asked Guy with his hand outstretched.

Cassie handed him the envelope. While opening it, he cleared his throat as if about to ask the most important question of his life or give the most important speech of his career. He reached for her hand to hold it as he read the card.

"I've written a few words that I would like to share with you.", he whispered and then began to read,

The majesty of my Queen is as noble as the Magnolia tree.

Her touch and love can heal the heart of any lonely man.

Her love strengthens the weakest of men and restores them to their majesty.

Her love is deeply rooted and immoveable when attached. I am but your humble and loving servant.

Cassie, my Queen, my heart is yours.

With all my love and devotion,

Guy Staton

Cassie released a gasp and collapsed into Guy's arms. He carried her to the sofa and he laid her down. He gently placed a pillow under her head. When she awoke, she had a dozen questions desperate to be uttered, like was he a cousin of KC or was he a half-brother to the illusive man? Fear and dizziness stopped her from asking the questions, but she was sure that her eyes revealed that she had many questions to ask.

"Cassie, are you alright?", asked Guy, "Do I need to take you to the hospital?"

"No, Guy. I guess my blood sugar dropped.", lied Cassie, "Can you pour a glass of orange juice for me?"

"Of course.", whispered Guy.

As he searched the cabinet for a small glass, Cassie's thoughts settled and her nervousness vanished. Had she known his connection sooner, she might have been able to seal the deal with Pink Staton. He might have revealed some information that she could have used against the bitch. Guy disrupted her thoughts when he returned with the glass of juice.

"Here you are.", Guy provided.

"Thank you.", Cassie said and then sat up to sip the unrequired juice.

"I'm sure it comes as a shock that I am a Staton.", Guy began.

You think, thought Cassie as she sat silently awaiting his explanation.

"I hate to lead with I'm a Staton if a woman isn't local. Most women hear that name and see dollar signs and wedding bells. They don't even try to get to know me after that. Don't even get me started on the local ones; their mothers have been plotting and playing matchmaker since their daughters came of age.", Guy explained.

His explanation left so many questions unanswered, but she knew that she would no doubt have to tread cautiously. She didn't want him to think she had known all that time and had been trying to use him; despite using his knowledge of the townspeople being the initial reason she even entertained going out with him. She had no idea that she would develop feelings for him. Feelings thought Cassie, exactly what are those feelings, she asked herself. She choked on the juice when she realized she had fallen in love.

94

"Are you sure you're well enough to meet my friends?", asked Guy.

Nothing would stop her, she thought, especially with that revelation looming overhead.

"Yes. Honestly, I am fine. I just should have snacked on something earlier.", Cassie lied again, "Let me put the flowers in a vase and then get my purse so we can head out."

"I can't wait for you to meet Pete, Pete's wife Carol, Tim, and Tim's wife Trudie. You already know Trixy.", Guy rambled.

The ride to Pete's home was slightly awkward with Guy talking nervously and Cassie being nervously quiet and afraid that she might say the wrong thing. She kept holding the pendant as she thought of Guy's connection to the Staton family. She was so tempted to ask about the powerful family again, but she bit her lip every time the thought crossed her mind. She had done it so much that she had a swollen lip. As the car approached the country manor, which she assumed was the home of Pete, she had never been so thankful to arrive anywhere. She hoped that the laughter of his friends would relax them both.

"Here we are! Let me get your door.", Guy blurted.

Guy cleared his throat as if to swallow his nerves; being nervous was not his usual mode of operation so he was determined to squash it. He quickly opened the door for Cassie who was still gripping the pendent as if her life depended upon it. He could see that she was still in shock from his revelation, but he didn't understand why it had such an immense impact on her.

"It looks like Guy and Cassie are here!", Pete exclaimed from a window.

"I will get that for you, Sir.", informed William Sherrod, the head butler.

"No, that won't be necessary. You and the staff are dismissed for now and can come back when it's time to clean up.", informed Pete, "Thank you, Sherrod."

Pete had been nervously waiting for them to arrive; it was not like Guy to be late. He was just as excited to meet Cassie as Guy was to introduce her. Cassie's presence in Guy's life meant the world to his friends because she was having a huge impact on him.

Until that point, Cassie had only seen the quaint side of the Staton and Raymond area. This was her first exposure to its wealth and she could see that for some, country living was very posh. She and Guy walked arm-in-arm up the stairs to the entrance. It was a two-story double gallery home; the upper balcony displayed beautiful plants and flowers sprawled near a comfy outdoor sofa. The manor was updated with white vinyl and a pink metal roof; everything else about the home screamed old money and history. A weeping willow was on either side of the house and flowers lined the flower beds around the manor. As they climbed the last step and reached the massive porch, Pete opened the door to greet them. Cassie barely had time to take in the beauty of the outdoor chandelier hanging overhead.

"Cassie! It's so nice to meet you. I'm Pete, a childhood friend of Guy.", Pete boomed.

He drew Cassie in for a hug which took her by surprise, although it should not have. Why would Guy hang around anyone less friendly than himself, she thought.

"Nice to meet you too!", declared Cassie.

"I was getting worried about you too when you didn't arrive on time.", Pete informed.

"Sorry about that. I gave Cassie a present and we got caught up in the moment.", chuckled Guy.

"All right now!", laughed Pete.

96

Cassie found herself blushing at Pete's implied reason for the delay, but Guy ate it up and shared a boisterous laugh with his old friend.

"Come on in. Cassie, everyone has been dying to meet you. Guy is so secretive, so you must be very special for him to want to introduce you to us, little people.", laughed Pete as he guided her inside from the foyer to the open gallery area.

Everyone had gathered there from the sitting room as they eagerly waited to be introduced to the lovely woman who had captivated Guy's heart. Cassie was again distracted from the beauty of the home by his friends.

"Yes, we are the peons!", declared Tim.

The rest of the group joined Tim's laughter.

"Don't mind that one!", joked Guy, "That's another childhood buddy, Tim Lockridge. We were so close as children, people swore we had to be family."

"If that was the case, I was the black sheep of the family.", teased Tim.

"You're not lying!", shouted Trixy.

Cassie observed that everyone laughed except the woman who stood alongside Tim.

"Cassie, let me introduce you properly to everyone.", Guy began and pointed, "Pete, as you already know is another childhood friend, and standing next to him is his wife, Carol Lowry. You already know Trixy. That's Tim's wife, Trudie. Folks this is the firecracker who has me wrapped around her finger."

"Hello, everyone.", Cassie smiled.

They all came near to hug her and welcome her to their fold.

"Staton men are crazy about strong women.", chuckled Trixy.

"Is that code for something, Trix?", laughed Tim.

"Watch it. 'Cause if that's true, you're barking up the wrong tree! Tread lightly!", laughed Guy.

Everyone laughed at Guy's warning as Cassie eyed Tim offering her own playful yet serious warning which made everyone laugh even more.

"Let's take this party to the sitting room.", Pete instructed.

Cassie finally had a chance to admire the beautiful gallery of the home. There was a beautiful staircase made of cherry wood with marble at the base of each step. It led to the upper gallery where similar to the lower gallery, there were framed pictures of family and beautiful paintings that looked priceless. As she and Guy followed Pete to the sitting room, they rounded a marble-topped antique Victorian parlor table with a plant in an Asian blue and white floral porcelain flower pot. The couple followed Guy's friends into the sitting room and through the tall Victorian door. Cassie had never seen a door casing as massive; it was original to the home and had a tall distinct crown molding with a transom to create a large door frame. It was regal and a fitting entry point for the elegant parlor.

Inside, Pete motioned for her and Guy to sit on the modern rendition of a Victorian-styled sofa. It was oversized with a tall back; the plush and thick cushioned sofas were placed across from one another with a genuine antique Victorian coffee table in between. Two plush matching chairs sat on opposite ends of the coffee table to create a boxed conversation setting. Although it was elegant, it felt masculine as the furniture and accent pieces were all in shades of brown. The softer elements were found in the paint color and the floor-to-ceiling drapes that were cream.

"Cassie, make yourself comfortable and help yourself to some appetizers before we have dinner.", informed Pete as he pointed to the coffee table.

"So, Cassie, you probably know more about us than we do about you. What do you do for a living?", inquired Tim.

"Damn Tim! Can she at least get comfortable on the sofa?", scolded Trixy.

"Trixy, it's no biggie. Tim, I could ask you the same thing because I don't know a thing about you.", teased Cassie.

"Ooh!', laughed Trixy.

"Well, damn. I don't know if I should be offended or answer the question.", laughed Tim as he continued, "I own a small engineering firm."

"He's being modest. He employs over 200 staff.", Guy boasted.

"Now back to Ms. Cassie.", laughed Tim.

"I'm actually on a leave of absence right now.", Cassie explained.

"Tim, I honestly don't even know, exactly what my Beautiful does.", Guy chuckled as he looked at her expectantly.

Cassie rested her hand atop Guy's hand as it rested possessively on her thigh.

"Dating Guy was the first time I didn't lead with that information. I usually would stand behind my title and success when dating.", Cassie confessed.

"I get it. It was my first time dating a woman without her knowing my ties to a prominent family, without the looming persona of the Staton family hovering over us. It was …", Guy paused.

Guy's friends looked from one to the other not understanding what Guy was truly saying.

"Refreshing.", Cassie supplied, "It was nice to get to know someone without any pretenses or expectations."

"Really?", Tim questioned.

"We've never talked about it. We've spent time talking about more important things like family, laughing together and ...", Guy explained.

"Having sex!", blurted Pete.

Everyone laughed at Pete's playful assumption as Carol's eyes scolded her husband.

"I'm serious. I know about the people who mean the most to her like her grandparents, her parents, and her Aunt Gloria.", Guy informed.

"True. And I know about his mother Rose, his sister, Gal, and of course Trixy.", Cassie admitted.

"Ouch!", Pete chuckled.

"You heard her. She knows about the really important folks.", teased Trixy.

"But seriously, our statuses aren't important. Can you believe, I just found out today that he's a Staton?", laughed Cassie.

"What the fuck?", laughed Tim, "He's not just any Staton; he's the one that holds the fucking keys to the universe in these parts. He's KC Guy fucking Staton III."

The laughter of Guy and his friends was deafening and Cassie felt another dizzy spell coming on, but she did everything in her power to cover it up with her laughter. The room seemed to spin as she realized that all along, she had been getting to know the man whom she believed to be illusive and untouchable. The man

100

who truly held the keys to the very thing her career needed the most.

"Don't let Miss Pink Rose hear you say that! She's got those keys in a death grip!", laughed Trixy.

Guy reared his head back in laughter as he gripped Cassie in his embrace; it was the only thing that prevented her from passing out. One more revelation and she was going to faint, fall forward, and hit the floor with a thud. She thought she was doing a good job at hiding her emotions, but Guy noticed that she looked pale.

"Beautiful, do you feel faint?", questioned Guy.

The curious and expressive eyes of his friends questioned his statement.

"Her blood sugar will drop if she doesn't eat enough.", Guy explained then reached for an appetizer, "Here Cassie, nibble on this wing ding."

Cassie gazed at the questioning eyes knowing they probably assumed she was pregnant. If she hadn't known the truth, she would have thought the same thing herself. She didn't know how she would get through the evening; the shock of it all was a heavyweight and almost too much for her to handle. Afterward, the entire evening was a fog; she laughed when she noticed others laughing and mirrored their expressions whenever possible. However, she had no idea what was being said; their words were like a foreign language to her as her mind swirled around the questions, she had for herself. Would she admit to Guy the reason for her business trip? Would he think she knew all along and was using him? Would she notify her boss that there was a conflict of interest and she needed to recuse herself from the deal? There was no way she could convince the man she loved, to sell his legacy for any dollar amount and there was no way that she ever would want that.

Chapter 7

Michelle had called Cassie at least three times that morning before Cassie finally answered; she was highly annoyed that Cassie had not called upon her return from the party. Cassie turned over in bed, looked at the ringing phone again, and reluctantly answered her best friend's call.

"What the fuck?", fussed Michelle.

"Good morning to you too.", Cassie said sarcastically.

"Why didn't you call me last night?", Michelle asked.

"Girl! I've been out of my mind since yesterday; getting dizzy and fainting.", explained Cassie.

"Bitch, you better not be pregnant; especially not by a broke cowboy!", scolded Michelle.

"Bitch, please, that would be the least of my worries. That *broke cowboy* as you put it, is KC Guy Staton III!", squealed Cassie.

"I know you're fucking lying! How did you find out?", shouted Michelle.

"At the party with his friends. His buddy Tim let the cat out of the bag.", Cassie informed.

"Awkward.", sighed Michelle.

"Who are you telling? Micki, I don't know how I missed it… Everywhere we went, it was like he was a celebrity coming in. I just assumed it was because the townspeople loved him so much.", confessed Cassie.

"Bitch, you had access to the solution all this time. You could have milked him for information and sealed the deal long ago, but it's not too late.", reassured Michelle.

"Bitch, yeah it is. I'm in love with him.", whispered Cassie.

"Oh, shit! For real?", questioned Michelle.

"Yeah, I was just as shocked as you when I realized it.", sighed Cassie, "But it can all blow up in my face if he thinks I was using him."

"Well … you were though.", laughed Michelle.

"Shut up! You know what I mean. I didn't know who he was though.", moaned Cassie.

"Well, you just need to come clean with him fast.", suggested Michelle.

"Fuck!", shouted Cassie.

"What?", asked Michelle.

"It just hit me that the bitch, Pink Staton, is his fucking mother!", moaned Cassie, "Why couldn't he just be Guy Staton a cousin or half-brother like I hoped after he told me he was a Staton."

"Wait a minute! I thought you said his friend, Tim, told you.", Michelle reminded.

"Girl, there is so much to tell you. I forgot to mention that before we left for the party, Guy gave me an expensive pendant and he read a poem that he wrote and signed the card, Guy Staton.", bragged Cassie.

"Okay, I need to do a video call right the fuck now!", insisted Michelle.

Cassie switched the phone call to a video call so that Michelle could see the necklace.

"Yes Bitch!", exclaimed Michelle, "It's beautiful."

"I know. I didn't take it off and I've been holding it in disbelief since he gave it to me.", giggled Cassie.

"You really hit the big time. I just googled his net worth and bitch …", Michelle gulped.

"What?", questioned Cassie.

"It's 700 million dollars!", squealed Michelle.

"Don't play games with me, bitch!", blurted Cassie.

"Naw, bitch, I'm not joking. You did good this time!", laughed Michelle, "Okay, does he have a brother … a rich friend?"

"Just a sister and his friends are all married except for Trixy. But she's not rich and you're not a lesbian.", laughed Cassie.

"If she had that type of money, I'd be her bitch!", shouted Michelle.

"Girl!", laughed Cassie.

Pete seemed thrilled that his best friend had finally found love; a genuine love that was not based on the millions Guy had in his bank account.

"I'm so happy for Guy.", Pete said as he snuggled Carol.

"Yes, he deserves a good woman who isn't out for his money.", whispered Carol.

She buried her face in Pete's chest hair as he kissed her forehead.

"But didn't it seem odd how surprised she was to find out his actual name.", remarked Pete.

"Wouldn't you be surprised? I know I would be too.", Carol defended.

"Yeah, but it was more … like she had … never mind. I might have read too much into it. I just hope she's as good for him as she seems.", Pete uttered then became distracted, "Let me get up. I forgot I need to make a call."

"Okay …", whispered Carol.

She watched her husband scurry out of the room to make the forgotten call.

"Fitzpatrick speaking.", announced Kenneth.

"I have everything in place to put the plan in motion.", announced the anonymous conspirator.

"So, what are you waiting for? I need this wrapped up ASAP!", demanded Fitzpatrick.

"Consider it done! I want this more than you do.", the co-conspirator confessed.

Fitzpatrick relished the idea of that victory; it would be the biggest deal of his career and he'd accept any offer that would make it happen. He contemplated how he would dismiss Cassie from the deal or if he should keep her attached should things go sideways and the company needed a fall guy.

"Hey … Guy.", Pete greeted. "What's up?".

"Hey, Pete. Are you in the middle of something?", asked Guy, "You sound a little distracted."

"Sorry Guy. I just got off an important phone call. I've got a situation that might be a little tricky, but enough about that. I want to know did your girl enjoy herself.", asked Pete.

"Yeah, she did, but it might have been information overload. I wanted to be the one that told her about my family ties and not one of you guys.", confessed Guy.

"Well, you should have told us that she didn't know. It's a little strange to me, but you do you.", laughed Pete, "Maybe she will be the one and you'll finally get married. To think there used to be a time I was jealous of you."

"Yeah, during your geeky days; I'm glad you eventually grew out of it. Thank God or you never would have won Carol over.", laughed Guy.

"True, but I think everyone was jealous of you at some point. I'm sure there are some sad fucks who still are.", laughed Pete, "You and Cassie are going to catch hell when you take her to some of the socialite events of the year."

"We are just living in the moment; although I've been drawn to her from the first moment I saw her. But she's from Michigan and will eventually go back home. If I want to pursue her, I'll probably have to do a lot of flying back and forth.", Guy explained.

"If you want it to work, you will find a way. You always get what you want.", laughed Pete, "Thank God, you didn't want Carol."

"Brother, she barely had a crush on me. She always talked about you when we hung out.", laughed Guy, "Truthfully, I think that she was just using me for information."

"So, that's how she got me wrapped around her finger. She knew all the inside information to reel me in.", laughed Pete.

"Sure, the fuck did.", laughed Guy, "You were so freaked out around girls. I had to help your geeky ass get one."

"What would I have done without you?", joked Pete.

"Be a lonely man.", laughed Guy.

"Well, just make sure *you* don't become one. Don't let Cassie slip away.", teased Pete, "Look, I need to let you go. I have an errand to run."

"Okay, no problem.", replied Guy.

Trudie had been pensive all morning and had come to a realization that had been staring her in the face for years.

"I can't keep up this charade!", Trudie confessed, "I'm tired of hanging with your friends and pretending everything is fine."

"What are you saying?", demanded Tim.

"I'm sick and tired of pretending I don't know about the secret phone conversations and fake nights away working. Your secretary slipped up and said you haven't been at the office after hours. I am not naïve; I know that you are cheating on me! You must be cheating.", protested Trudie.

"You are snooping and checking up on me?", questioned Tim.

"There's nothing else to discuss. I want a divorce!", insisted Trudie.

"Are you sure that you want to give all this up and go back to your mother's trailer?', Tim smugly questioned.

"Right there, your true colors! You had me fooled that you were a knight in shining armor to protect and provide for me. But you are a snake! A low self-esteemed snake that thinks your possessions give you the value and worth you've wanted since childhood. Tim, you need help, sooner rather than later.", shouted Trudie.

"I don't have time to listen to the psycho-babble of trailer trash.", Tim dismissed his wife and left the room.

Later that day the conspirator decided he needed to find someone desperate enough for money to help put his plan into action and the best place to go was the poorest rural town near Staton county, Grey Creek. He took the route off the main highways into the small town in a neighboring county. Many residents were so desperate for cash, that they would be willing to sacrifice their freedom for the right price. The plotter entered the local convenience store and spotted a derelict attempting to buy beer but coming up short.

"Here, let me take care of that for you.", offered the stranger.

"Thanks, brother. I'm Hank.", Hank obliged.

Hank extended his hand to the stranger who stared at it and remained nameless before he whispered.

"Looks like you could use some extra income.", suggested the conspirator.

"How you reckon?", joked Hank, "What type of work do you need done?"

Hank could tell that money was no stranger to the newcomer. He was willing to take whatever offer he could find that would prevent him and his pregnant wife from being evicted from their trailer. Subsequently, he followed the stranger outside the store.

"Do you have a vehicle?", probed the stranger.

"Yeah, that pick-up truck over there.", Hank pointed out.

"I need you to drive to Staton Farms' cow pasture today and inject this in one of them.", the stranger informed.

Hank took the small tackle box from the stranger and opened it to find a syringe inside.

"What's in this?", questioned Hank.

"Nothing dangerous to you.", the stranger informed, "I'll give you five thousand after it's done."

"How would you know it's done?", Hank inquired.

"Trust me, I'll know. Do we have a deal?", the stranger urged.

Hank realized for the first time in his life, that he was sitting on a goldmine and finally had the upper hand. If the stranger could pay five thousand dollars without batting an eye, he could pay ten for the job.

"I'll take ten thousand dollars.", Hank announced with an outstretched hand.

"Okay, it's a deal, but you will get paid once the job is done. Do it today and meet me back here a week from today at the same time.", instructed the stranger.

As the conspirator drove off, he felt that finally his family would be avenged for the wrongs they had suffered at the hands of the Staton patriarch, KC Staton Jr. He hoped that small, yet dangerous act, would weaken the farm enough to make Pink and Guy second guess their decision not to sell. Once that disease spread through the farm, he would suggest one more act to seal the deal for RQ Acquisitions.

Cassie and Guy had plans for a date that evening. He had originally suggested that they go horseback riding that morning on his property, but she insisted he take her out on the town to a fancy restaurant instead. There was no way she would agree to go to Staton Farms before she had confessed her intentions for coming to town. Cassie dreaded the day she would have to meet Pink Rose; she hated that the locals used nicknames. If the bitch and the sexy cowboy had gone by their first names, then she would have known from the start who he was.

She would look at things through a different lens now that she knew his real identity and she would be able to appreciate the reactions of the townspeople and waitstaff. When she thought Guy was a farmhand, she accepted that they would never dine at expensive restaurants, unless she were willing to foot the bill. Finally, she had a reason to wear the one formal dress she packed. She pulled the silver sequined halter gown from the closet. She knew she would be stunning in the piece; its deep V-neck and hip-high slit were eye-catching and would drive Guy crazy, she smiled as she examined the garment. She imagined Guy not being able to resist touching her exposed back or not touching her period.

Cassie laid the dress on the bed and pulled out a pair of Tom Ford silver leather padlock sandals with a metal heel. The metallic leather was the perfect look to compliment the dress without distracting from the elegance of the dress. Her body tingled as she thought about her upcoming evening with Guy. Perhaps she needed to touch herself before she saw him because her nerves were on edge. That was the quickest way to relax her and she wanted to be relaxed as she made her first debut among the area's elite.

Pink Rose had a nagging feeling that she was not through with Ms. Williams. She had decided to relinquish her desire to handle the situation and allow Guy, the true head of the company, to deal with her. Perhaps, he would have better luck. Pink Rose headed to Guy's bedroom to update him on her decision when he burst from his bedroom.

"Where are you off to?", questioned Pink Rose, "I was hoping to discuss business. I want you to handle the acquisitions firm instead of me."

"I have a date with the second most important woman in my life.", announced Guy, "I need you to put a pin in that thought for later. I don't want to be late picking her up. We're dining at the Legacy."

"I hope you are at least letting Mr. Henry drive you instead of going in that monstrosity of a truck!", insisted Pink Rose.

"Of course, mother. There's no reason not to.", insisted Guy.

"Good. We'll discuss business later. And I hope you introduce me to your lady friend soon.", Pink Rose shouted to her son's back.

Since the cat was out of the bag, Guy figured he might as well put some of his wealth on display for Cassie and there was no more perfect way than letting Mr. Henry drive him in the Rolls Royce. Henry stood at the bottom of the stairs in wait for Guy.

"Guy, you look dashing. You inherited the best from your parents' people. Your father's good looks and your mother's height. Your lady friend is a lucky one.", complimented Henry.

"No, Mr. Henry. I'm the lucky one. She's one of a kind. I can't wait for you to meet her.", exclaimed Guy.

"Well, we better get a move on it. The Legacy frowns on late reservations; no matter who you are.", laughed Henry.

Guy looked at his Rolex and nodded before jogging out the front door. With each stride, his suit strained against his muscled frame. He was striking in his navy blue suit. It was a tri-blend of linen, wool, and silk with tan stripes. The tapered pants hugged his thick thighs. He was the perfect picture of a modern-day Southern gentleman; he wore black loafers without socks as was the trendy style of the day. He had changed his hairstyle by asking his stylist to give him a tapered haircut leaving a long curly mane on his crown that he put in a man bun.

"Guy, wait! Let me open the door for you.", insisted Henry.

Henry was much too old to jog to the car as Guy had and needed the younger man to wait for assistance. Henry eyed the young man; he felt all the fatherly pride that KC Jr. would have felt if he were still alive. Henry felt that Guy needed to settle down and he hoped this lady friend would be a perfect match. As the pair drove to Cassie's place, Guy eyed the gift box and the bottle of champagne chilling on ice.

"Henry, do you think I'm doing too much?", asked Guy.

"Guy, with all due respect, you haven't done enough.", laughed Henry, "City girls are a little different … trickier than country girls. If you don't show your affection enough to her, she might slip out of sight!"

"Well, I can't let that happen.", chuckled Guy, "No, a woman like Cassie only comes once in a lifetime."

Cassie was bubbling with excitement and nervousness as she fussed over her appearance in the mirror until eventually, she sought the approval of her ride-or-die, Princess.

"Princess, how do I look?", asked Cassie as she twirled.

"Woof!", barked Princess.

"I think I look sexy as hell too.", laughed Cassie as she eyed her shoes, "But Guy definitely will have to help me into the truck."

"Woof! Woof!", barked Princess as she charged toward the entrance.

Cassie gathered her evening purse and followed Princess to the entrance where she found Princess jumping and wagging her tail excitedly. Cassie shooed Princess away from the door as usual so that she could greet her man. Her man thought Cassie, her nipples hardened at the thought as she quickly opened the door. Seeing him in the past did not prepare her for the Adonis who faced her. She did not think he could be any sexier, but there he was fine as fuck, she thought; all she could see was him. Cassie was blind to anything else. She allowed her gaze to soak him in as she eyed him from head to toe and back up again. She unknowingly purred as her eyes devoured him before she possessively kissed him.

Guy loved her aggressiveness and he along with his body would do anything their Queen demanded of them. But he wasn't about to let Cassie forget that he was powerful and any control she had over him was because he relinquished it to her. He commanded that control when he lifted her slender frame and slipped his hand up her dress to claim the treasure, he knew was fully bare and exposed for his touch. Henry cleared his throat as the young couple he assumed had forgotten they had an audience.

"Excuse me, Sir. Remember your reservations; you are cutting it awfully close.", Henry reminded.

Cassie was startled by that authoritative voice that appeared from nowhere when she realized the familiar truck was not parked out front but a Rolls-Royce instead with a driver. Guy noticed the surprise in Cassie's eyes and was excited to flaunt the once-hidden information about his wealth.

"I thought I would deliver on my promise to pay for everything and now since the truth is out … I can really show off.", chuckled Guy, "Come let me introduce you to Henry. He's a longtime employee but more like family."

Cassie closed the door behind her and allowed Guy to lead her to the car by her hand when she noticed the driver's familiar face. Shit, she thought, she never thought about the driver being someone who knew her true intentions for coming to town. What if he told Guy? Cassie's body became stiff as she robotically walked to the car with Guy. Henry's eyes made contact with hers. Cassie hoped that Guy would not notice the surprised expressions on her or Henry's faces as that was not how she wanted to explain her actions.

"Henry, are you okay?", Guy questioned.

"Yes, of course, Sir.", Henry informed.

Guy didn't understand Henry's reaction; he questioned whether or not Henry's reaction was based on Cassie being Black. He had not thought it was necessary to describe her as such. Henry and Cassie recognized that uncomfortable look in each other's eyes as they realized they knew each other.

"Henry this is my girlfriend, Cassie. Cassie this is Henry, my lifelong supporter and confidant."

"Nice to meet you.", whispered Cassie in a seemingly coy way.

"The pleasure is all mine. Guy, you told me that Ms. Cassie was one of a kind, but I didn't know she would be this beautiful.", Henry complimented.

Guy reached to open the door.

"Sir, let me get that for you.", insisted Henry.

Guy tried to assist Cassie into the car first, but Henry insisted that Guy enter first so that he could assist Cassie instead, then Henry whispered in Cassie's ear.

"Not to worry, Ms. Cassie. I'm just an employee. I don't interfere in the Staton family's personal affairs.", assured Henry.

Henry began the short drive from Raymond to Staton; he hoped to get the couple to the Legacy on time. He couldn't resist looking at the pair in his rearview mirror; after being introduced to Cassie and previously seeing her in action, Henry knew that Guy's feelings were genuine. Nevertheless, he hoped the beauty was not playing some end game and was using the heart of the gentle giant to bring the family empire crashing down.

Despite his fears, Henry believed she was everything Staton men loved, strong-willed, sexy, aggressive, and powerful. The days and months ahead would be quite entertaining, thought Henry and he was glad he would have a front-row seat. Guy saw Henry smiling in the rearview mirror and Guy assumed that Henry's approval was the only reason for the smile. Afterward, Guy felt that evening was getting off to a near-perfect start and wanted it to continue.

"May I?", asked Guy as he held the bottle of Champagne and a glass.

"Yes, please.", Cassie replied.

Cassie was thankful for the alcohol and hoped that it would relax her nerves. Cassie accepted the glass and was about to gulp it down to prepare for a refill when Guy presented her with another gift box. Thank God for the gift, thought Cassie; her nervousness might have gotten her drunk, and then her lips would have gotten loose.

"Guy ...", Cassie purred.

"There's nothing too great that I wouldn't do for you.", declared Guy.

Cassie nervously opened the box; it was something about the presentation of his gifts that gave her goosebumps and made her think he was about to propose. She quickly removed the ribbon and opened the box to reveal a Rolex watch that matched his own. It was a customized watch with a mother-of-pearl with diamonds on the dial, a diamond bezel, and a diamond-encrusted platinum president-style bracelet.

"Oh my God.", Cassie whispered.

"Let me put it on for you.", offered Guy.

Cassie was shocked; she had never dated anyone on his level before and her last *boyfriend* flaunted his imitation Rolex as real. She hated that the fake-it-till-you-make-it lover even came to her mind; he was her past and this new future was very bright! Had anyone told her that her spring fling or fuck would become the love of her life, she would have cussed them out and told them to go to hell. But there she was, in love for the first time in her life and scared shitless that she would lose him. Guy was humbled that the fierce and fearless Cassie, Queen B, was close to tears. He leaned closer and pulled her into his arms to whisper the words his heart felt the first time he saw her.

"Beautiful, I love you.", Guy whispered.

"Cowboy ... I love you too.", Cassie whispered hesitantly.

Guy devoured her lips and Cassie's body went limp in his arms. She felt protected in his strong embrace and knew he would be her defender. It was the first time, she ever wanted to be vulnerable or weakened by love. She completely trusted him to accept her at her strongest or weakest moments and she vowed she would never lie to him again if he forgave her for the truth she had yet to reveal. Despite her fears, their evening together would prove that fear had no place in her mind or heart that evening. She felt like Cinderella at the ball; every eye was on her and her dashing date as they waited to be seated by the host.

"Hello, Miss. Welcome back, Mr. Staton. It has been a while since you've attended with your mother.", informed the maitre d', "Now I see that you have been preoccupied with other things."

Guy chuckled, "Yes, I have. Charles, this is my girlfriend, Cassie Wiliams."

"Nice to meet you.", Charles affirmed, "Right this way, please."

Charles directed the couple to the middle of the restaurant and sat them there for all to see and ponder who the mystery lady was in whom Guy delighted. Guy assisted Cassie with her chair as Charles dismissed himself.

"Enjoy. Your waiter will be with you momentarily.", Charles informed.

"This place is so refined. Based on the name, I was expecting a converted plantation house or something.", joked Cassie.

"Oh no, I wouldn't have sprung something like that on you.", laughed Guy.

"If you had, it would not have been pretty.", laughed Cassie.

"Oh, I know.", laughed Guy.

Guy squeezed her hand and then held it possessively.

"This is my uncle's restaurant; it belongs to my mother's oldest brother.", Guy explained.

"Oh, so you are a blue-blood on both sides of your family tree?", teased Cassie.

"I don't know how noble we are, but wealthy yes.", laughed Guy.

There was her cowboy, the genuinely humble man whose confidence and self-worth were not defined by his power or wealth. She appreciated a man who did not flaunt his power and accomplishments; the ones she dated in the past who did that were either fraudsters or arrogant pricks. Either way, she despised them and everything they represented. She credited those types for molding her into a cold-blooded woman when it came to dating; she dated men the way most dated women, until now.

Everything about their date that evening was surreal: the attentive waitstaff, the way the elite patrons acknowledged Guy and the elegant restaurant. Above it all was the dashingly handsome man who sat across from her. Guy had changed up the whole game for her, her entire way of being actually and she hoped she would come out on the other side better and stronger for it.

However, if one is not careful others will attempt to manipulate situations to fit their goals and desires and undo everything done to create a better life. Hank knew that very well and his current situation was no different. He didn't comprehend the reason the stranger wanted him to inject the contents of the syringe, but he knew doing so would guarantee him the much-needed payday that he had only dreamed could happen. Hank spotted one lone cattle that lagged behind the others and had not been secured for the night. He was all too comfortable snooping around in the dark; his mother always said he had eyes like a cat and could see anything under moonlight. Like the feline, he was quiet and light on his feet; his thin frame moved quickly and quietly closer to the cattle until he was close enough to release the substance. The beast groaned at the unexpected pinch of the needle and then ran off to join the rest of the herd.

Hank ran from the pasture into the woods toward his truck; as he ran, he envisioned the pleasures he would do with his newfound wealth. Under the cloak of night, Hank slipped inside his car and sped away from the scene. He doubted he would sleep much in the coming days until he met with the rich stranger to get the thousands promised to him. The night was surreal for him as he eyed the tackle box that housed the now empty syringe; he would come out a richer man for it.

Chapter 8

"Good morning, Ma.", Guy greeted.

Pink walked to the serving buffet along the dining room wall to pour a cup of coffee and grab a bagel and fruit.

"Yes, it is. It's such a beautiful Monday morning, a great way to start the week.", agreed Pink, "I'm surprised you aren't out and about checking on the livestock."

"No, I'm a little exhausted.", chuckled Guy.

"I just bet you are!", smirked Pink, "I haven't seen you much all weekend. Were you with your girlfriend?"

"Yes. I can't wait to introduce you.", announced Guy, "In fact, I want to do it soon, maybe next week. I will ask Gal if she can come to town and the staff can show out for my girl."

"We haven't hosted a fancy dinner in a while. I can even make her a special figurine.", exclaimed Pink.

Pink was ecstatic; Guy had never brought home a girlfriend to introduce to the family. So, she knew this one had to be special and would more than likely be her future daughter-in-law. She carried the cup of coffee and plate to the seat next to Guy.

"I am so happy for you. She must be something special.", acknowledged Pink.

"She truly is. You two are so much alike.", laughed Guy.

"Oh, my! You told me that once before.", laughed Pink, then she became serious, "I wish your father were alive to see this day. He would have been so proud and happy for you."

"Yes, Ma. Me too, but his spirit lives on, here in this house and on this land. I feel his presence every day as I work among the farmhands and tend to the animals.", admitted Guy.

"Yes, I do too. That's why I fight so hard to keep the Staton family legacy alive and strong.", confessed Pink.

"I know Pa knows.", Guy consoled, "My future children will have you to thank for preserving the family's legacy."

Chip bursts into the dining room out of breath and flustered.

"Excuse me Mrs. Staton … Guy", began Chip.

"What's wrong?", questioned Guy.

"I've been trying to reach you most of the morning, but your phone has been going straight to your voicemail.", Chip panted.

"I'm sorry. I guess I forgot to take it off 'Do not disturb'.", informed Guy, "What's wrong?"

"The cattle are getting sick.", began Chip.

"Sick?', Pink interrupted.

She feared the worst as no one had complained of any possible virus in decades.

"Calm down, Ma. Let Chip finish.", Guy insisted.

"On Saturday we noticed a few sick cattle; now, the numbers have grown to at least thirty. The hands are isolating any that look sick. Whatever it is, it's spreading like wildfire!", bellowed Chip.

"Calm down. Ma, wait here. I'll let you know what's happening after I get more information.", persuaded Guy.

He placed his hand on Pink's shoulder as reassurance that he would get to the bottom of the matter and then he stepped away from the table to accompany Chip.

"Chip, walk with me and tell me anything else you know. Has the doctor provided any updates?", insisted Guy.

"We are waiting for the test results ...", Chip gulped.

Pink remained behind as Guy had instructed while the two headed to the barn. Something didn't sit well with her; the farmhands and staff had always been so careful in identifying sick animals to prevent outbreaks. She did not trust that this was a natural occurrence and prayed that Ms. Williams did not have a hand in it. She was tempted to contact Ms. Williams with the accusation but opted not to reach out.

The secret that Cassie was hiding was weighing very heavily on her heart; she was frozen in fear whenever she contemplated telling Guy the truth. She knew the truth was bound to come out, but she was petrified to inform him and to see the hurt in his eyes. One thing for certain and two things for sure, she needed to call her boss and recuse herself from the deal; if she didn't Guy would never forgive her and their relationship would go up in flames.

"Hey Fitzpatrick.", Cassie hesitantly greeted her boss.

"Ready to come back from your leave?", questioned Fitzpatrick.

"About that ...", Cassie began, "Yes, I am but I plan to work remotely from here for a bit. About the Staton deal ... I need to recuse myself from it. I've become too attached to the townspeople and ..."

"Don't worry about it; there's no need to do that. Your name can remain attached so you will get your commission once the deal is done for the hard work you've already put in. We're very close to closing the deal and I intend to ensure you get *all* the credit for it.", Fitzpatrick informed.

"Really? I don't understand...", Cassie questioned, "Mrs. Staton seemed so opposed to the offer."

"Yes, but all the pressure you applied is starting to pay off.", lied Fitzpatrick, "Look I have another call coming in."

That was the oddest conversation she had ever had with Fitzpatrick; it was nothing for him to remove her peers from a deal, so she pondered what was so special about her situation. Maybe a fun conversation with her girl would help her think more clearly to figure out his angle; so, she decided to call Michelle.

"Michelle! What's up?", greeted Cassie.

"Not much, girl. I *need* to ask you that question.", laughed Michelle, "Lately, I've been experiencing life through your stories."

"Yeah, right! You know that you always have guys begging to take you out on the town and to spend their money on you.", laughed Cassie.

"You ain't lying, but none have that money like Guy!", laughed Michelle, "So why is your voice so heavy?"

"Well for starters, I've got to tell Guy about my job and the reason for coming to town. And I tried to get my boss to remove me from the deal, but he wouldn't.", informed Cassie.

"Yes, you've got to tell Guy the next time you see him. And who the fuck does Fitzpatrick think he is?", fussed Michelle.

"My boss... that's who.", blurted Cassie, "He has someone else finishing up the deal, but said he would leave me attached for the commission."

"When has he ever cared about looking out for you? If that had been the case, you would have received another promotion or at least been assigned to all the big deals.", theorized Michelle.

123

"Exactly! That's why it seemed odd and he said my replacement is close to closing the deal so he wants me to get paid for my earlier efforts.", informed Cassie, "I don't know how to feel about it."

"Well, whatever Fitzpatrick has planned is going to make *your* shit hit the fan if you don't come clean with Guy. So, don't let anything stop you from telling it all to Guy; unless you don't really want him.", Michelle warned.

"Bitch, you know I want him! I am so stressed. No matter what I do, I might lose him, the fuck!", screamed Cassie, "I should have told him when we left the party."

"Well bitch, it's too late for should have's, could have's and would have's. You better do something quickly.", scolded Michelle, "Don't wait for him to ask you out. Invite him over and try to cook something … better yet hire a traveling chef. Like I said, it smells like shit is about to hit the fan hard and you need to be prepared and ready."

"I do need to be more proactive about this thing. I've been extremely reactive of late and that's not like me.", confessed Cassie, "I'll check online for a cook and invite the cowboy over."

"Good. I really need you to seal the deal with Guy and then find a rich one for me.", laughed Michelle, "I don't care if it's an old uncle or his great grandpappy on death's door! I don't give a fuck which one; just find me one, bitch!"

"Bitch, please!", laughed Cassie, "The universe threw Guy in my lap. You better ask my Auntie Gloria for help."

"Girl bye! Your auntie will have me hooked up with a deacon of her church. He'll have me wearing dresses to my ankles with nothing exposed but my face, hands, and feet. Nobody's got time for that shit!", hooted Michelle.

"Girl, her picks aren't that bad.", giggled Cassie.

"Did you forget about Trustee House?", sniggered Michelle.

"Oh, shit! You're right, bitch! I forgot about him. Okay don't ask her.", hollered Cassie.

"Okay, bitch! You see my point!", laughed Michelle.

"Thanks for the laugh and good advice as usual. Let me check on a chef and see if my cowboy can come over.", informed Cassie.

"No problem girl. Talk later.", Michelle laughed.

Guy and Chip stopped by the barn after putting on hazmat suits as a precaution. Guy was close to tears as he witnessed the effects of the unknown illness wreaking havoc on the livestock. He had never seen or heard of anything this severe. A voice on the intercom overhead paged and informed Guy that the doctor was there and he was needed in the conference room in the main office building. Guy wanted to hold on to any hope that the doctor had identified the cause and had a treatment plan.

"Let's go!", ordered Guy.

"Yes, sir!", informed Chip.

The two left and headed back to the building to remove their suits. Guy wondered what his father would have done in a situation like that as he hoped to grasp strength and knowledge from his father's past leadership. As he and Chip entered the main conference room, he received a call from Cassie.

"Hey, how's my sexy cowboy?", asked Cassie.

"Beautiful, I wish I could say I'm doing great, but we have an all-hands-on-deck emergency at the farm. Can I get back to you later?", explained Guy.

"Sure, baby.", Cassie reassured, "Make sure you do, so I know you're okay."

"You got it beautiful.", promised Guy, "Sorry everyone, I had to take that call. Doctor, what do you know?"

"Well, sir; how do I put this?", the doctor hesitated.

"As plainly as possible.", instructed Guy.

"Sir, this is not a natural virus commonly seen on farms. It was most likely created in a lab and your livestock were infected with it.", disclosed the doctor.

"What the fuck are you saying?", asked Guy in disbelief.

"This was a biochemical attack, sir.", explained the doctor.

Guy's face, neck, and hands turned a crimson-red and he could barely see as his anger boiled. He questioned who would stand to gain from an attack other than the acquisition company; surely, they would not be that devious, but his mother had warned him not to be dismissive of the threat. He could hear his mother's voice urging him to get more involved. The doctor noticed that Guy and the rest of the staff needed reassurance that they could contain the threat.

"Fortunately, I was able to secure a treatment that you should give to the infected livestock and the others as a vaccine to prevent infection.", the doctor informed.

"So, are you saying that we should be able to save our livestock?", inquired Chip.

"Indeed! There might be one or two of the infected that have become too weak to survive even with the treatment, but the rest should be okay.", the doctor explained.

"What are we waiting for? I want the cattle treated immediately no matter the cost. We can't risk a cross-species infection!", ordered Guy.

"I took the liberty of bringing the treatment and you can order more if it isn't enough.", the doctor informed.

"Good man. Will there be side effects?", inquired Guy.

"Possible. I would keep the infected permanently separate from the rest for observation. You may want to use them for breeding purposes only or sell them for their cowhides.", the doctor advised.

"I see. Well, thank God, at least we contained it so it shouldn't have a devastating effect on our business... Let's get to it!", Guy demanded.

Everyone left the conference room determined to save the cattle and Guy remained furious because he had to address the invisible elephant in the room, the acquisition company and he would insist that he would be the one to do so. When he had decided to leave the conference room and follow the staff, he received two incoming calls back-to-back, one from Tim and the other from Pete. He sent Tim's call to voicemail and reluctantly answered the next call.

"What the fuck!", Guy shouted before answering the call.

"Pete, what's up?", barked Guy.

"Hey, I didn't do it!", laughed Pete, "I'm just calling because you're late for our golf game."

"Hell! Bud, I'm sorry. We have an emergency here. Cows are coming up sick as fuck. I'll get back to you later.", insisted Guy.

"Sure thing. We'll talk later.", Pete suggested.

After disconnecting the call, Guy sent a text message to Tim informing him of the issue so that Tim wouldn't call back wondering why he hadn't answered. Instead of hovering over the staff during the treatment, he decided to go back to the house to update his mother and to put a plan in motion to handle the firm that was no doubt to blame for the scare. When he entered the study, he saw his mother pacing the floor and squeezing her hands together.

"If that bitch is responsible for this, I'm going to ring her fucking neck!", shouted Pink.

"And I won't stop you.", assured Guy, "Although violence would feel good at the moment, it's not going to solve our problem."

"Is the doctor able to help?", Pink worried.

"Yes, he has a treatment plan and the staff are giving it to the cattle as we speak.", Guy reassured.

"Thank God!", Pink sighed, "We've got to do something about that company. I know they had something to do with this."

"Yes, I agree; but we need to find proof or some other dirt on this company to either press charges or take them to court."

"I told you to take that company seriously ...", Pink began.

"At this point, none of that matters now. We have to come up with a plan of action. Before their threats appeared to be just bravado, but when someone attacks my legacy, I take it as attacking my family.", barked Guy as he slammed his fist on top of the portable bar cabinet along the wall.

Pink became fired up again when she saw the sleeping bear awakened; Staton men were jovial, and gentle until someone attacked what they held dear. That's when the beast appeared and got shit handled; she couldn't wait for him to bring Ms. Williams down several pegs until she begged for forgiveness.

Guy fixed a drink and gulped it down as he thought about Cassie. Perhaps, he could brainstorm a resolution with a relaxed mind and the only thing that could relax him was Cassie holding him in her arms.

"Ma, I need to be with my girlfriend right now. We'll talk later.", Guy informed.

"I understand.", Pink assured.

Guy kissed his mother on the cheek before leaving the room. He had never just shown up to Cassie's place without being invited, but now was not the time for formalities. He needed his girlfriend and if he were honest with himself, it was time that he made her more than that. Guy decided he would swing by the cabin before heading to see Cassie.

Pink knew that if Guy's girlfriend were anything like her as he indicated, his girlfriend would give Guy the pep talk he needed to ignite his fiery nature that he kept subdued. Pink couldn't think of anything else to do; she was at her wit's end with Ms. Williams; it was up to her son now.

Guy drove his truck swiftly to the cabin and made two calls before arriving there. Now was not the time for the farm to experience a potentially catastrophic attack as he could envision the perfect life with Cassie. The crisis at the farm almost made him feel powerless and it was not a feeling to which he was accustomed. There was one thing he could take control of and that was letting Cassie know he wanted her to be a permanent part of his life. He was determined to secure the farm's financial viability for their future so he and Cassie would have a legacy to give to their children.

Cassie was a nervous wreck; she wanted to call or text Guy to ask him over, but she didn't want to seem shallow or selfish during his crisis. Despite not securing a chef, she was about to call him when she heard a knock at the door. She wondered if it was Guy; however, she noticed that Princess was curious but did not display the excitement she normally reserved for Guy's arrival. So, it must not be his truck that pulled out front. She quickly walked to the door to see who could be stopping by unexpectedly; when she opened the door she saw a delivery person.

"Ma'am, I have a delivery for you.", informed the young deliveryman, "Where can I sit them?'

"Them?", asked Cassie.

"Yes, Ma'am!", laughed the young man, "Your boyfriend must be crazy about you. I have about five more arrangements to bring in and the largest one has a card on it."

"Oh yes... that's my cowboy.", blushed Cassie.

There was no way she would let their next time together end without her telling her truth. He deserved that and so much more, thought Cassie as the young man brought in the arrangements. Each one seemed desperate to outshine the previous one.

"This one here is a big'um.", laughed the deliveryman.

His thin frame struggled to carry it inside; he placed it on the island next to the rest. Cassie had begun to spread them out and put them throughout the living space and dining area. She removed the card from the largest arrangement and started to read it as she escorted the driver out.

"You mean everything to me, Cassie. You are my joy, my strength, and the love of my life. See you soon. Love, KC Guy Staton III.", whispered Cassie as she read the card aloud.

Princess barked as if she understood and approved of Guy's words.

"I know, girl.", sighed Cassie, "I stumbled upon a good one. Our Auntie would say that God placed us right where we needed to be to meet him."

"Woof!", barked Princess.

After showering and dressing for his surprise visit to Cassie's place, he opened the antique trunk that once belonged to his grandmother. He searched the bottom of it beneath other heirlooms to find the small box that held one of the many things his dear grandmother wanted him to pass on to his future wife and children.

"There you are.", whispered Guy.

He sighed as he opened the small box to reveal his grandmother's wedding set. It was six karats of perfection in platinum; the large solitaire diamond was surrounded by emerald-cut diamonds that curved above the shoulder like a bow and more down the shoulder of the ring. The gallery sat high with more diamonds on the bridge; the accompanying band had a filigree bridge with diamonds atop its triangular point and shoulder. Despite not being Cassie's bohemian style, he felt she would appreciate its sentimental value and accept it as a part of him, her cowboy.

It was time for Guy to put everything in motion; he felt that once he took control of his personal life the rest would also fall in order. Unknown to the conspirator, the farm was attempting to rebound from the attack. He had heard of the attack's success, but did not know the actions Guy and his staff had taken to recover; so, he was on top of the world and decided to drive his rental to the small town early in search of Hank. He hoped to find Hank at the same spot where he met him and sure enough, he could count on the drunk to be right where he hoped he would be. He spotted Hank's old rundown pickup truck outside the convenience store; he parked and waited for Hank to come out. He watched Hank gingerly walk toward his truck. It was quite apparent Hank had a hangover and that he would soothe it with more booze. The conspirator quickly exited his car to get Hank's attention.

"Hey.", summoned the conspirator.

Hank's eyes lit up like a Christmas tree as his mouth watered for booze he could buy after he paid his late rent. He stumbled over to the stranger as quickly as he could.

"Here for your trouble.", offered the stranger as he held an envelope," I threw in an extra two grand for the good job you did!"

"Thanks, brother!", Hank responded as he snatched the envelope excitedly.

"I may have another job for you soon.", indicated the conspirator, "Where do you stay?"

"On Old Twelve Way off of Beaver Dam.", Hank offered, "We are the only trailer on that road. You can't miss us."

"That's easy enough to find. I'll be in touch soon. Don't spend it all in one place.", smirked the stranger.

Just as sure as the conspirator was that victory was within reach, so was Guy that he would overcome the latest challenge. Statons of old did not back down from a challenge or bow out gracefully and Guy was just as determined; he already had a plan and would put it in motion first thing in the morning. So, for now, thought Guy, Cassie was his only concern. Guy arrived at Cassie's rental home as the florist drove away from the property. He was thrilled that he thought to surprise her that way; although it was nothing near the way he had imagined proposing. He wanted to fly her somewhere on his private jet and make the moment unforgettable, but now that would have to take a backseat. The crisis taught him, if nothing else, that he needed to seize the moment and not wait for the *perfect* time because it may never come.

Guy tapped his pocket on his plaid shirt which Cassie often teased him about; he wore the very thing that garnered him the nickname cowboy. He was so rushed to go to her that he didn't take the time to put on anything special. He wore a plaid shirt, jeans, and his work boots; he chuckled when he realized it. Oh well, he thought, that was him and she had come to love it.

Cassie inhaled the beautiful scent of the flowers and couldn't wait to hear from her man. She wanted to hold him, kiss him, and beg his forgiveness. Suddenly, Princess started her familiar bark and dance whenever Guy came; shortly after, Cassie heard a truck pull up the drive. She became just as excited as Princess and skipped to the door to see if it was indeed her cowboy. She opened the door to see Guy resolute in his steps, but his eyes told her he was worried and drained. She was determined to revive him before she broke her news. Cassie flung open the door before Guy could ring the bell.

"Beautiful ...", Guy began.

Cassie's kiss interrupted his greeting. She felt the tension in his shoulders as she gripped his body. Things must be worse than she had imagined as she had never felt his body so tense. She would focus on relaxing and pleasing him before she said a word. Guy obeyed her unspoken orders as he followed her to the bedroom with Princess barking and jumping behind them. Cassie's attentiveness reminded him of what his father often said, 'A man with a strong, attentive, and loving woman supporting him can accomplish anything.' He finally understood what his father meant as he allowed Cassie to remove his clothing. He slipped out of his work boots so she could easily assist him in removing his pants. He was expecting her to stand so that he could kiss her passionately, but she had another kiss in mind. She confidently gripped his manhood and tasted every inch of it before attempting to place it completely in her mouth. She gagged because she couldn't do it; the sound of her attempts aroused him even more.

Guy couldn't restrain his desire; he needed to feel her breast and taste the sweetness of her body. He pulled her to her feet and lifted her maxi sundress over her head to reveal her nakedness. He effortlessly lifted her and carried her to the bed, but before placing her on it; he buried his head between her legs to taste her. Cassie moaned not only because of the strength of her man but due to the immense pleasure he always gave her.

"Woof!", barked Princess.

"Get out of here!", cried Cassie.

She had intended to sound stern with Princess, but the sensations coursing over her body made the words almost unutterable.

"Guy …", moaned Cassie.

Guy devoured every inch of her hidden treasure as he carried her to the bed and then he flipped her over to lay her down on her stomach. He smothered his face between her buttocks as she moaned and cried his name over and over again. Cassie was accustomed to being the aggressor during their love-making, but her cowboy showed her that he was the one truly always in control. He made love to her as if she was his and would never be claimed by another and all those who came before him meant nothing. He flipped her over to devour her more and when his manhood entered her, Cassie was out of her mind with orgasm after orgasm. Her body shook from his powerful thrusts; thrusts that seemed determined to rip through her uterus. She could feel his tension dissipate with each passionate thrust. As his body pounded her harder and deeper, the louder Cassie's moans and cries of passion became until they both climaxed together. Princess barked from the living room when she heard Guy's animalistic groans.

"Yes, cowboy; the fuck!", Cassie exhaled, "Ooh, baby …"

"Shit woman! Do you realize what you do to me?", moaned Guy.

Guy turned over to lay on his back and pulled Cassie close so she could rest her head on his chest. Cassie knew that was the perfect time to discuss her secret. She knew men were their most susceptible during pillow talk and she knew she needed all the help she could get to receive his acceptance, but before she could utter a word, Guy began talking.

"Beautiful, it's overdue for you to meet my family. I am planning a dinner with my mother's help for the following weekend so I can show you off to everyone.", Guy beamed.

"That's wonderful Cowboy, but I need to talk about the acquisition company.", Cassie began, "Have you thought about just selling to them? You can focus on your other endeavors if you do and besides, I've heard that raising cattle damages the environment."

Cassie wanted to slap herself; she had no explanation for sidestepping her confession. Perhaps it was fear, she thought, but she couldn't pinpoint it as she had never feared anything before falling in love with the cowboy.

"Beautiful … that's ridiculous and you are much too intelligent to believe that lie. Mankind has farmed and raised livestock since the beginning of time.", Guy defended, "I don't understand why you are discussing this now. What's going on?"

Guy was baffled as to why she was discussing the acquisition company instead of focusing on the fact that he wanted to introduce her to his family. He kissed her on her face and lips to distract her from that conversation, but she seemed hell-bent on continuing it for some reason.

"Sorry, I'm fumbling around the real subject I need to discuss…", whispered Cassie, "I guess I'm nervous for some reason."

"You, nervous?", laughed Guy, "Never!"

Guy kissed Cassie passionately and felt that he should propose then. Perhaps that would give his queen the strength and trust to confide in him whatever was burning to be said. He remembered the ring was in his shirt pocket that had been tossed aside. He did not want to disturb the flow he was trying to create by getting up; that would open the door for Cassie to mention the acquisition company again. Instead, he called Princess.

"Princess!", shouted Guy.

Cassie looked at him confused and semi-annoyed that he would call her back to the room. Princess came running and stood in the doorway waiting for instruction from her new best friend.

"Girl, bring my shirt.", instructed Guy as he pointed.

Princess did as she was told.

"Good girl. Now git!", ordered Guy.

"Look at that bitch!", laughed Cassie, "If I had told her that she'd still be staring me down. Why do you need your shirt? I know you aren't leaving."

"No Beautiful, I am not leaving.", Guy replied as he removed the ring box.

Cassie's heart almost stopped when she saw him remove the box from his pocket. You better not be playing with me cowboy, she thought. Every thought of her confession fled from her mind as she watched Guy climb over her to the floor where he kneeled on bended knee at her side. She sat up still in shock at what appeared was about to happen. As he opened the box, his eyes never left her gaze. She saw so much love in his eyes; it reminded her of how her father often gazed at her mother when he kissed her goodbye before leaving for work. Never in a million years did she believe she could find someone to love her like that.

"Cassie, you are one in a million.", smiled Guy, "I still can't believe you want me, Beautiful, but I'm thankful. Will you marry me and allow me the honor of loving you, and providing for you for the rest of my life?"

Cassie's hard exterior vanished as tears rushed down her cheeks and Guy kissed them away.

"Yes, Cowboy ... yes Guy ... yes KC Guy Staton III! I will marry you!", squealed Cassie.

Guy slid the antique ring on her slender finger and then picked her up to kiss her. Cassie held her arm outstretched as she squealed with excitement causing Princess to come running back to check things out.

"Guy, it's stunning!", gushed Cassie.

"I know it's not your style, but it belonged to my grandmother, Caroline. I hope it fits okay I didn't have it sized or anything.", Guy explained.

"It fits perfectly and it's perfect because it's from you.", beamed Cassie.

The couple cuddled in bed after the proposal and it led to more kissing and lovemaking. Cassie's bravery returned and she knew now more than ever the urgency to confess her actions to Guy. She inhaled deeply as she buried her face in his chest.

"Guy.", Cassie began.

"Yes future Mrs. KC Guy Staton III and the lady of the manor.", chuckled Guy.

Oh my, thought Cassie, that would be another battle when she confronted the current lady of the manor and dethroned her. She inhaled deeply and pushed that thought to the rear recesses of her mind.

"I never explained my work to you and why I even came to town.", Cassie commenced.

"I know.", laughed Guy, "Pete still jokes about that."

"I'm an executive with ...", Cassie paused.

Guy's cell phone rang and interrupted Cassie's confession.

"Don't answer it, baby.", pleaded Cassie, "This is more important."

"No, I have to. The farm was attacked some days ago and livestock are sick.", Guy explained.

Cassie had no idea and now completely understood why he had been so stressed. She was surprised he could keep it together as well as he had.

"You've got to be fucking kidding me!", shouted Guy, "I'll be right there!"

"What's wrong baby?", inquired Cassie.

"My men just spotted people on the property. That fucking RQ Acquisitions has orchestrated another attack on the farm... I'm sure of it! Fuck!", bellowed Guy.

Guy ran his fingers through his hair to dig his nails into his scalp out of frustration and then decided to put it in a bun.

"The acquisition company ... what?", Cassie questioned.

"Beautiful, I'll explain more later. I've got to go. Those sons-of-bitches better pray to God that I don't find them first because I'm going to shove my rifle up their asses!", threatened Guy.

Cassie was in a fog after Guy's words; it was as though she was watching a movie scene play out as she watched Guy gather up his clothes from the floor. There was no way that Fitzpatrick had taken her suggestion seriously and put it into action. That must have been the real reason to keep her name tied to the project so that she would be the fall guy, she feared. Fitzpatrick planned to set her up should things go wrong, she thought.

Guy dressed and kissed her lips before rushing out. She barely recalled it and when she came to her senses, she had no idea how long she had been sitting naked on her bed staring at the beautiful engagement ring.

"What are you going to do now, bitch?", she asked herself.

Chapter 9

Cassie had tossed and turned all night long and when she did manage to fall asleep her moans and groans startled Princess, which had caused her to come running to lay her head on the bed alongside Cassie's. As a result of a restless night, Cassie woke up tired and with a massive headache. She had nightmares of being put on trial and prosecuted for a crime she had not committed. She could still hear Pink Rose Staton yelling at her and calling her a scheming bitch. Cassie's mouth was dry as a powder house; who even knew where that saying originated, thought Cassie as she dragged her body to the kitchen to pour a glass of water.

Waking up after a night of incredible lovemaking and a proposal should have been euphoric, but instead, fear and panic were attempting to settle in. Cassie couldn't take her gaze off the stunning engagement ring; the weight of the diamonds seemed to weigh a ton and she couldn't stop staring at it and twisting it. She drank the water and without thinking, she slammed the glass down on the countertop.

"Fuck!", screamed Cassie as the glass shattered, "Shit!"

Cassie immediately began cleaning up the mess she had made; she prayed she would be able to clean up her biggest mess just as easily before it got out of hand. It might have been too late, she worried. Perhaps she should call Micki, she thought, then she rushed immediately to the bedroom to retrieve her phone and dialed her confidant.

"Bitch, pick up!", Cassie yelled at the phone as she waited for Michelle to answer the video call.

"Bitch, do you know what time it is?', Michelle complained, "I was trying to get a little more sleep before my alarm rang. This is my day to go into the office."

140

"Sorry I can't sleep ... anyway Micki, forget about that! Look at this, bitch!", Cassie insisted.

Cassie held her left-hand ring side up in front of the camera.

"What the fuck is that?", questioned Michelle, "I know you're fucking lying. That pussy *must* be 'real' good. He proposed even after you confessed to him?"

"Naw, bitch. I haven't told him yet!", cried Cassie covering her face with her diamond-adorned hand.

"Shit, girl! You're fucking up and just keep digging a bigger hole for yourself.", Michelle warned, "What are you waiting for?"

"Who the fuck knows? But honestly, each time I was going to tell him last night he interrupted me. First, it was him interrupting to propose to me. I beat around the bush so much while I tried to confess, that he fussed at me for bringing up the acquisition company. Then I attempted again after more lovemaking, but someone called him from the farm.", Cassie rambled.

"Why would his staff call him late like that?", questioned Michelle.

"That's the whole problem. That son-of-a-bitch, Fitzpatrick put a plan in action that I told him as a joke. He had someone to attack the cattle and many of them are sick. And then last night Guy's staff spotted people on the property again.", chattered Cassie.

"I knew that bitch ass Fitzpatrick was up to something!", shouted Michelle, "You're just going to have to blurt it out to Guy."

"I'm scared that I'm going to lose him ... I've never been afraid of anything.", confessed Cassie, "I don't know how to deal with this."

"Well, bitch, like I told you before, you might lose him either way you play it. I know you don't wear panties, but you've got to put on your big girl drawls and tell him!", scolded Michelle.

"I have two battles ... even if Guy forgives me ... that bitch of a mother is going to give me pure hell.", admitted Cassie.

"Oh, yeah bitch. Get prepared; it's a sure bet she will.", Michelle warned.

Guy had a restless night after he left Cassie's place; however, unlike her, he had been up all night. Upon his return home, he and his crew formed a search party and combed through the acreage for hours until they stumbled upon a group of boys who were having a party in one of the original barns. It was another sign that 'Mother knows best'; Pink had suggested they tear down the old fixture or refurbish it if they let it remain. But he had ignored that just as he had ignored her warning about the acquisition company. It was just one of many requests of his mother that he had ignored and perhaps he would finally learn to take heed.

As soon as the boys had been spotted, Chip called the police. Guy and his crew loaded the guys into the pickup trucks and then drove the teenage boys to one of the offices to interrogate them before the police arrived. He had been determined to get to the bottom of it all.

"Why the fuck are you on my property? Did you poison my cattle?", demanded Guy.

His voice boomed in the silence of the night and his tall frame loomed over the young men as he demanded a response. His voice, stern expression, and the flexed veins and muscles in his neck warned them to take him seriously. Perhaps they were mistaken for thinking the easygoing Guy that the townspeople spoke so well of would let the incident go; instead, they saw a man that towered above them like an intimidating force. One decided that he would be the spokesperson for the group.

"Mr. Staton, we were just trying to have a private place to have fun, drink, and share some laughs without our folks riding us.", confessed Joey.

"Yeah, sir. We eat your products at my house. I wouldn't do that.", insisted Charlie, another boy brave enough to speak.

"I hope to God you are telling the truth because if I find out any of you are lying, I will fucking beat the shit out of your asses. And I don't think you can handle that shit.", Guy's voice boomed the warning.

Later, Guy sat in the study with a cup of coffee and contemplated the night's events; he had just finished the police business concerning the boys. He had called the parents of each teen and promised he would not press trespassing charges this time, but if he found them on his property again, they would get a beating and face charges. He told the parents, teens, and anyone within earshot that if they had been men, he would have shot and would have asked questions at their hospital beds later. The parents had vowed to keep a closer watch over their teens and some were willing to volunteer their sons for free labor if Guy wanted. Guy denied their offers and advised that work is honorable and should not be used as a punishment.

Pink entered the study and interrupted Guy's thoughts; from the look of his worried frowns, he must have been thinking about the night's events.

"Guy, I missed you at breakfast. Are you sure you don't want me to whip something up for you?", asked Pink as she walked toward her only son.

"Sorry about that; I'm good.", Guy held up his coffee, "I'm sure you were expecting an update so that you can weigh in.", Guy appeased.

"No, that's not why I said that. Pooh Bear, I only ran the company all these years because I felt you were too young at the time of your father's death. But now, you are more than capable … this is your legacy.", Pink explained.

"I thought you enjoyed running the company … that it gave you purpose.", Guy contended.

"Yes, sweetheart, I have enjoyed it; however, my only purpose was to ensure your legacy remained intact. Staton Holdings, Inc. is yours and yours alone.", insisted Pink, "I'm now here for support and nothing more."

She touched his wrinkled brow with the back of her hand.

"I'm fine, Ma. I'm just stressed nothing more.", chuckled Guy thinking she was feeling his forehead for a fever.

"I know. I just hate to see those worry lines.", Pink explained, "You know … the family could use some good news right now."

"Well, I actually have some good news that we can focus on.", Guy informed.

"What's that? Have you forced the acquisition company to back down?", Pink concluded.

"Hopefully soon, but that's not it. I proposed to Beautiful last night and she accepted!", chuckled Guy, "I can't wait for you to meet her."

"Guy! I'm so happy for you. Soon, I'll finally be able to say I have grandchildren.", giggled Pink.

Guy loved to see the softer side of his mother and he delighted in the idea of her spoiling and showering his children with love.

"I must plan something special for the dinner now that she's my future daughter-in-law. Did you mention the dinner to her? I know we have a lot going on, but this will be good for all of us!", Pink rejoiced.

"Yes, I did. Did you contact Gal already?", asked Guy.

"I did, but you know how she is with me. She doesn't answer if she thinks I want to make demands of her.", sighed Pink, "You better call her if you want her to come."

"I'll make sure I give her a call later today.", promised Guy.

"Sounds good. Well, I'll let you relax and I will start ordering items for the dinner slash engagement party. Should I keep it simple?", inquired Pink.

Pink knew he was not flashy and preferred simplistic things, but she desired to splurge on the event.

"The sky is the limit; you have full reign to plan it as you see fit. Have fun!", chuckled Guy.

"Wonderful!", exclaimed Pink.

It took Cassie all morning to motivate herself to get up, dress, and eat breakfast. She realized that despite keeping Michelle updated while she was in Mississippi, she had barely spoken to her mother and auntie. This was definitely a good time for a call, she thought. She immediately dialed the two ladies by video call.

"Hello, doll.", greeted Gloria, Cassie's aunt.

"Hey, Auntie.", greeted Cassie, "I added Mommy too."

Gina, Cassie's mother, joined the call next.

"Hey, Baby Girl. Hey Gloria.", greeted Gina, "Gloria and I were just saying the other day that we haven't heard much from you at all."

"Sure did.", added Gloria.

"I'm sorry about not calling...", Cassie apologized.

"How's it been going with you? I hope you haven't been too bored down there in the country.", inquired Gina.

"Bored? Not at all. This assignment has been kicking my ass. Oops sorry, Auntie.", Cassie admitted.

"Doll, don't mind me. I hear my younger friends cussing all the time.", Gloria reassured.

"What do you mean by kicking your butt, Baby Girl? You usually love the tough assignments.", inquired Gina.

"True, I usually do. But this owner, part owner … whatever title she has … has given me the flux, and then to top it all off I fell in love with her son unknowingly.", moaned Cassie.

"Fell in love?", questioned Gloria.

"Wait … what?", squealed Gina.

"Yes, you heard me correctly. I'm in love and engaged to get married.", exclaimed Cassie.

She threw her hand in front of the camera so they could see the brilliance of the diamond ring.

"Oh, my God!", shouted Gloria, "Thank, Ya!"

"I can't believe it!", cried Gina, "You said you never wanted to get married."

"Well, that was before Guy changed the game for me.", laughed Cassie.

"God and a good man will do that!", giggled Gloria.

"I don't know if God did it, but Guy is a damn good man!", laughed Cassie.

"Amen.", sighed Gloria.

"I'm just so happy and ... that ring! It's beautiful.", complimented Gina.

"Yes, it is!", agreed Gloria.

"Thanks. It belonged to his maternal grandmother. She wanted him to give it to his bride-to-be.", informed Cassie.

"So, if he's the company's owner, he must be rich!", squealed Gina.

"Yes, loaded! I mean old money rich.", Cassie boasted.

"A rich man's proposal is something, isn't it?", laughed Gloria, "Everyone I know is marrying a rich man. Hell, where can I find one?"

Gina and Cassie laughed at Gloria's response.

"If any woman deserves one, it's you, Auntie Gloria.", Cassie praised.

"Yes, that's true. I do believe yours is coming soon.", Gina prophesied.

"I'm just teasing. Never mind me. We need to focus on this upcoming wedding. We have all sorts of planning to do.", Gloria emphasized.

"Yes, we do.", Gina paused and contemplated, "He really is a good man to propose knowing you were trying to convince them to sell."

"Yes, a truly understanding man.", added Gloria.

"Um ... yeah about that.", Cassie began, "He doesn't know yet. It's a mess waiting to happen."

Gloria and Gina were stunned and stared at Cassie in disbelief.

"I know …", sighed Cassie as she covered her face with her hand.

"My Lord!", sighed Gina.

"Jesus!", cried Gloria.

"I know … I know.", groaned Cassie.

"We don't need to tell you what you need to do. It's obvious.", Gina provided.

"Yes, Lord.", added Gloria.

"I just been so afraid to tell him.", admitted Cassie.

"Afraid?", questioned Gloria.

"When have you ever been afraid?", laughed Gina until she realized her daughter was serious.

"Well, you've come too far to freeze up now. The next time you see him, tell him and make that happen sooner rather than later.", Gloria ordered sternly.

"Yes, Auntie.", sighed Cassie as she had done since a child with her favorite aunt.

"Well, your auntie and I have things to discuss. So, we will talk to you later, Baby Girl.", explained Gina.

"Handle your business, doll!", insisted Gloria.

"Okay, Mommy … Auntie. I love you old chicks.", giggled Cassie.

"Bye!", the elders said in unison.

The small towns near and around Raymond, Mississippi had not seen as much action in years. For almost two weeks, the townspeople of Staton were abuzz with talks of the events, some rumors, truths, and fabrications; but all of it was entertaining.

Word of the events even made its way to Grey Creek. Hank heard the rumors and forfeited his instructions from the stranger. He didn't want to taunt fate; he had already made more money for a job than he had ever dreamed possible. He was money-hungry, but he wasn't starving, he thought.

Hank left home and was heading into town to get his weekly supply of liquor, but thanks to his newly found wealth, that was his second visit for the week. After turning onto the main highway from his dirt road, he noticed a slowing vehicle heading his way with the wealthy stranger in the driver's seat. No doubt he was in the area to see Hank. Hank pulled over to the side of the road and waited for the stranger to pull up behind him. The stranger exited his car and approached Hank where he stood at his car lighting a cigarette.

"What are you doing here?", asked Hank.

"You don't remember I said I would have another job for you?", the conspirator questioned, "But I haven't been able to track you down; it's like you're dodging me."

"Yeah brother, I do remember ... I was just hoping you wouldn't.", confessed Hank.

"What are you talking about? You don't want to get paid?", asked the stranger.

"Brother, there is too much heat around Staton Farms. People say the Statons have armed guards patrolling their land. It was easy to do the job the first time, but now, there are just too many eyes.", Hank educated.

"Look, I'll give you 20 thousand dollars if you do this next job for me.", offered the stranger.

"Brother ...", Hank moaned.

Hank's mouth watered at the thought of 20 grand in his hands. He wasn't sure if it was worth the risk because of all the attention placed on the property at the time. Hank thought about the possible outcomes; he could get arrested before getting paid. An equally bad outcome would be getting arrested after the payoff and his old lady spending the money on her new man.

"Another job ... no, I better not press my luck. As you can see, I'm not that lucky.", laughed Hank as he pointed to their surroundings.

"Just think of what you can do with 20 grand.", the conspirator tempted.

It didn't take much to persuade Hank. He thought he would be a fool to pass up that type of cash; besides he had done dumber things for less, he thought.

"Fuck.", sighed Hank, "What do I have to do?"

"It might be a two-day job ...", the stranger began.

"I want half up front or I'm not doing it.", Hank demanded.

The conspirator was slightly annoyed by Hank's bold request, but he guessed Hank had earned the right to make demands at that point.

"Okay, you've got a deal. I'll bring the money tomorrow along with the tools for the job.", the stranger reluctantly agreed, "This is what I need you to do ..."

Chapter 10

Time seemed to be in express mode and was moving faster than ever. It had been a week since Cassie spoke to her mother and auntie and promised to be honest with Guy. She had failed at that promise; each time she looked at his saved contact information, she chickened out and did not call. Whenever he called or texted, she discussed everything but her hidden truth. She was in a real bind because she was a day away from the huge dinner that Guy's mother planned for their engagement announcement. She was thankful that Guy had promised that the guest list was only comprised of family, and the gathering would be small. If things blew up in her face, at least the whole town wouldn't know right away.

Cassie had worn almost every outfit worthy of being presented to the Staton clan, so she had convinced Jill to step away from her shop to go shopping with her. Cassie drove her vehicle leisurely into town; she had become accustomed to the slower pace of life. Surprisingly, the city girl, in her, did not miss the hustle and bustle of city life at all. She could imagine shopping and having dinner with Jill after they finished their workday or Jill joining her and the kids at a park. Cassie blushed as she acknowledged her thoughts drifting to little Staton babies. Perhaps, that could never be her reality if Guy did not forgive her. The daredevil in her, or was it the devil, reassured her that Guy would forgive her and she could hold off longer or wait until she confronted Pink Rose herself.

Cassie pulled up in front of Jill's boutique and parked. She thought she would have a chance to go inside and look around at Jill's new inventory, but Jill bounced out the door ready to roll.

"Hey, girlie!", exclaimed Jill.

"Hey girl!", laughed Cassie.

She always wondered how Jill would react if she greeted her the same way she did Michelle. She decided that she would test it out one day for a good laugh, she thought.

"Ready?", Jill asked as she hugged Cassie, "My mother is tending the store for me."

"Great. I was hoping to step in and say hey.", Cassie informed.

"She'll still be there when we come from Sammie Jo's", laughed Jill.

"Okay smart ass.", laughed Cassie.

"Come on Sammie Jo is waiting.", Jill fussed.

"Alright, but I hope she has some nice outfits.", Cassie worried.

"Yes, she told me she deliberately ordered some things you might like.", Jill informed.

"I wonder why. I guess everyone wants a piece of the out-of-towner's money.", laughed Cassie.

"That … and I might have slipped up and told her that you and Guy are getting married.", Jill confessed, "Please don't be angry. Sammie Jo is as quiet as a church mouse; she promised she won't say a word to anybody."

"Yeah right. We'll see.", sighed Cassie.

Cassie playfully poked Jill's shoulder as the two giggled down the sidewalk to Sammie Jo's shop. Before the two ladies entered the shop, Sammie Jo spotted them approaching from her window view. She immediately rushed to the entrance to greet them.

"Congratulations Cassie!", squealed Sammie Jo.

Cassie looked at Jill with an annoyed and piercing stare.

"Quiet as a church mouse, huh?", whispered Cassie sarcastically.

Jill shrugged her shoulders at Cassie and bypassed her to hug Sammie Jo.

"Isn't it exciting!", giggled Jill.

"Yes, their wedding will be the biggest event in the region. Ms. Cassie ...", Sammie Jo said out of respect for her upcoming status, "I want you to know that I design gowns and dresses here also; the only thing I order is the trendy styles. I would be honored to design your wedding dress."

"Just call me Cassie and thanks for the offer, Sammie Jo, but we don't even have a date set yet.", Cassie blushed.

Jill hugged Cassie and whispered to her new good friend.

"You better get used to folks catering to you. You'll be practically royalty around these parts.", giggled Jill.

"Okay, girls follow me over here.", Sammie Jo instructed.

Sammie Jo pointed to the rack of dresses toward the back of the store near the fitting rooms. Cassie had never visited Sammie Jo's boutique before; she had assumed she would only find old-fashioned mammy-made outfits. However, she was pleasantly surprised by the simple elegance of the boutique. Cassie smiled as she approached the tri-fold mirrors outside of the fitting rooms.

"Girls, you can sit and make yourselves comfortable. I have some white wine for sipping if you like.", Sammie Jo informed.

She pointed to the cocktail serving table alongside the oversized plush gold chairs as she walked toward it. She poured the ladies each a glass of wine and passed it to them graciously before proudly walking to the rack of dresses. She presented her favorite one to Cassie.

"Cassie, this one is adorable. I know it isn't your bohemian style, but it is the perfect summer dress for the future queen of Staton Farms.", beamed Sammie Jo.

Cassie agreed that the dress was not her style, but she did see its appeal. It was a summer white maxi dress with a V-neck bodice and an empire waist cinched just below the bust. The soft fabric cascaded down with oversized flower petals; the petals were in shades of mauve, white, and gold. Cassie stood and reached for the supple fabric.

"It's perfect.", smiled Cassie.

"Wonderful!", squealed Sammie Jo, "Okay, go into that fitting room and I'll bring you the perfect sandals to match."

Sammie Jo beamed like a proud momma as she carried the rose-gold leather belt buckle sandals to Cassie's fitting room. It was a 4-inch heel sandal with a mock belt buckle across the vamp of the sandal and a thick buckle around the ankle. She gently knocked on the door to get Cassie's attention. Cassie cracked open the door and leaned out.

"Here are the perfect sandals. I can't wait to see the finished look!", exclaimed Sammie Jo.

Jill was clapping, bouncing, and squealing as she sat on the plush chair waiting for Cassie to exit. Cassie beamed as she exited the fitting room. She was stunning in the dress.

"Well?", asked Cassie as she twirled.

"Gorgeous!", boasted Sammie Jo.

"I don't know ... There's one thing that needs to be adjusted.", suggested Jill.

Cassie and Sammie Jo looked perplexed and annoyed that Jill didn't think the dress was perfect. Cassie stood with her hands on her hips waiting to hear Jill's complaint. Jill approached Cassie and adjusted the deep V-neckline to show more cleavage.

"You know you show more cleavage than that. Who are you trying to fool?", laughed Jill.

Cassie and Sammie Jo hollered as Jill adjusted the bodice to reveal Cassie's best assets. Cassie shimmied her breasts for the ladies.

"Exactly!", laughed Cassie, "Guy loves them!"

The ladies laughed uncontrollably. Sammie Jo and Jill beamed as they saw the joy in Cassie's eyes. Everything was leading up nicely to the marvelous dinner that Pink Rose had planned. Even Guy felt the excitement in the air as he visited the stables. He placed his phone on silent to silence the outside world. If there was an emergency, the staff could easily reach him and Cassie never called during the morning hours; so, any received calls were unwanted.

Guy smiled as he went on his morning horseback ride on the farm. The warmth of the sunlight beaming down warmed his body and thoughts of Cassie's love warmed his heart. Despite facing challenges, he felt assured that with Cassie by his side, he could eliminate every threat to their empire making it stronger than ever. When he returned to the stables, he noticed his mother marching inside and from her stern expression, he knew things were not good. He increased his horse's gallop and entered the barn.

"Ma, wait!", Guy urged, "What happened?"

Pink Rose closed the stall and turned to address her son as he put his mare in her stall.

"I decided to confront the firm ...", sighed Pink Rose as she threw up her hands apologetically, "I know I said it was in your hands, but you know me. So, I called and asked for the bitch, but instead, I was transferred to Mr. Fitzpatrick who informed me that my contact was on leave from the case. And there was nothing to discuss and the next time we talk will be after we sign the paperwork that will arrive soon."

"What the hell!", Guy's voice boomed, "That arrogant son-of-a-bitch. Did he say anything else?"

"No, that was it and then he hung up!", fussed Pink, "I need to calm down and clear my head; that's why I was going to ride."

"You don't have to worry about that prick; I'll handle it. You have more important things to focus on. So, relax and enjoy your ride.", Guy smiled.

Guy approached his mother and then pulled her into his arms. He knew that she had been just as stressed, if not more so than he; her life's work had become protecting his legacy and she would feel like she had failed her late husband if she did not. Guy kissed his mother on her cheek and sent her on her way. The RQ Acquisitions staff's arrogance made him more determined than ever to show them how stubborn and tough a Staton can be.

As the day wore on, Pink Rose and Guy put Fitzpatrick and his threats on the back burner where they burned to ash as they focused on the final details of the dinner for Cassie's big reveal. During the evening, Cassie tried countless times to reach Guy but he did not answer her calls or text messages. She had finally found the courage to confess her truth and the man wouldn't answer her calls. She assumed everything was fine and perhaps he was following behind his mother making sure everything was perfect for tomorrow evening. Tomorrow evening would be explosive if she didn't confess everything to him before being escorted into the mansion.

That night Cassie welcomed sleep; however, she was tortured by nightmare after nightmare as she attempted to sleep. She tossed and turned as she moaned in agony during her nightmares. Just as she was being tortured in her sleep, Hank was on a mission to inflict more turmoil on Staton Farms. He took the supplies and instructions from the wealthy stranger and did as he was told. The stranger informed Hank that the previous attack was too small-minded and should have been grander. Hank attempted to execute the grander scheme as he ventured inside the farm's water refinery to release toxins. This time, the stranger's plan would affect any beast or man that consumed the water supply.

Hank had been extra cautious and moved stealthily in the night on the grounds, but the heightened security systems registered his movements notifying grounds security of his presence. Chip had been putting in extra hours as he was confident that another attack would occur at any time. When the security systems alerted Chip and the staff, Chip instructed the armed security to check out the water refinery and he would notify the family. Chip jumped in his truck and drove to the mansion farther into the compound.

Although Guy's night had been restful, he was awake and contemplative as he lay in bed thinking of Cassie. His peaceful rest was disturbed when Chip ran inside the house yelling for him to come downstairs. Boy barked with the same intensity as Chip and rushed from Guy's open bedroom to hurry down the hallway. Guy imagined the worst; he panicked and jumped from the bed. He ran through the hallway to the stairs in search of Chip.

"What the hell happened?", demanded Guy as he rushed down the staircase.

"Our security system picked up someone at the water refinery.", explained Chip.

Guy was astonished that someone would go to that extreme to destroy everything his family had built.

"To do what?", Guy questioned.

"It looks like the man attempted to poison the water supply.", fumed Chip.

"Fuck!", shouted Guy.

Pink Rose eventually stirred from her sleep after she had heard Guy's pounding footsteps down the hallway. She rushed from her bedroom barely securing her robe in her haste and entered the foyer where she heard the tail end of the conversation between the two men.

"Those sons-of-bitches!", screamed Pink Rose.

Pink Rose ran into the study to pull the rifle from the wall, and Boy barked frantically behind her. Guy followed her inside the library to take the rifle from her grip.

"No, Ma. Let me handle this.", Guy pleaded.

Although he wanted to unload the rifle in the man's ass, he needed questions answered and a corpse can't talk. As Guy removed the rifle from his mother's grip, the call came on Chip's walkie-talkie indicating that they had captured the man. Pink and Boy were on ten and desperate to follow Guy.

"Ma, stay here; you too Boy. Chip, let's go get that son-of-a-bitch!", growled Guy.

Guy and Chip ran from the mansion and hopped into Chip's truck; they sped off to the north end of the farm not far from the water refinery where the guards were holding the suspect.

"Give me your two-way.", ordered Guy.

Guy contacted the guards to provide instructions.

"Scott!", called Guy.

"Yes, sir. We got the son-of-a-bitch. We are about to call the police.", advised Scott.

"Hold off until I get there. I need that bastard to answer to me first. Damn it!", shouted Guy.

"Yes, sir!", complied Scott.

Chip and Scott knew exactly what that meant; it was time for Guy to shed his nice guy persona so the suspect could meet the beast beneath the surface. He spared the previous trespassers because they were boys, but this one was likely responsible for the first attack and he would receive every bit of the ass-kicking he was due. As Guy and Chip approached the men, Guy could see the pathetic excuse for a man in handcuffs kneeling on the ground begging to be released. Guy's menacing six-foot-four-inch frame exited the truck and he walked deliberately to Hank.

"Mr. Staton, I beg you, sir. This wasn't my idea. I just needed the money.", cried Hank.

"I know. You don't look smart enough to think of any plans this elaborate.", Guy determined, "Who had you to do this?"

"I don't know his name. He just offered me a shitload of money and I'm fuckin' broke so I took it.", Hank cried, "Please I just did ten years in the clink."

"Prison is your last worry.", Guy informed as he pulled Hank to his feet.

Guy's eyes turned menacing and Hank knew what he could expect to follow that gaze. Guy formed a fist and began punching Hank in the gut and his face before pushing Hank to the ground.

"Again ... tell me who put you up to this shit! What was the Northerner's name?", demanded Guy.

Hank looked confused at Guy's accusation that implicated a Northerner.

"It wasn't no Northerner. He was from these parts.", provided Hank, "I swear ... I don't know nothing else!"

159

Guy sneered at Hank and lifted him once again to his feet.

"I swear Mr. Staton!", whimpered Hank.

Guy ignored the man's cries for mercy and began beating him to the ground once again until Chip called Guy's name to spare Hank's life.

"Guy!", yelled Chip, "Sir, we should call the police now and let justice be served."

"No.", sighed Guy as he caught his breath, "I won't press charges. Look at him. Life has beaten him enough. He's a pathetic man- toothless, broke, reeks of alcohol, and ignorant. Release him. I want to find the fuck who paid him to do this!"

Guy took Hank by the collar to give a final warning.

"But if I catch you on my land again, I promise I'll kill you.", threatened Guy.

"I swear I won't do this shit again. I won't even come near these parts, I swear!", cried a bloodied Hank.

"Now get the fuck off my land!", shouted Guy.

Hank dragged himself as fast as his pain would allow him back toward his vehicle. Guy's eyes never left sight of the broken man as he slowly walked away.

"I want guards on duty 24/7 until I bring the bastards behind this down.", ordered Guy.

"Yes, sir. I'll begin creating a schedule immediately.", Chip reassured.

"Good, I don't want my fiancée to be frightened or worried about any of this shit. I need this handled once and for all.", Guy disclosed.

The men looked at one another astonished as they had no idea that their boss had proposed to his girlfriend or that he even had one. The men quickly dismissed their surprised expressions to focus on their assignment as they did not want to be on the receiving end of Guy's anger. The men nodded and promised to be vigilant. Chip and Guy entered the truck so that Chip could drop Guy off at the mansion to provide as much rest as possible before the big day ahead.

Despite getting up during the middle of the night, Guy was up at the crack of dawn and did his normal morning routine. He checked with each foreman regarding their specified area such as cattle, chickens, pigs, and other operations on the compound. He was relieved that everything seemed in order; it was a normal day on the farm for those unaware of the previous night's scare. When he checked back in at the house, he noticed that his mother was supervising the decorations and place settings for the dinner. He was glad she was focused on the engagement dinner, something hopeful and nothing else.

"Good afternoon, Ma. Sorry, I didn't check on you this morning.", Guy apologized.

"Pooh bear, that's okay. I spent the morning in reflective thought and prayer. It was the only thing that seemed to calm me.", Pink explained.

"I'll be glad when we overcome this challenge.", Guy admitted.

"Yes, me too. The family hasn't experienced an attack on our legacy in nearly a hundred years.", Pink contemplated, "And we didn't cave in then and we won't now."

"That's for damn sure. But you just continue focusing on the dinner. I can't wait for you and my Queen to meet.", smiled Guy.

"Queen? Your father used to call me Princess. She must be something if you've elevated her to queen status.", laughed Pink.

161

"You have no idea, but I actually call her Beautiful. Queen is somewhat of an inside joke.", laughed Guy as he began to walk away.

"Guy, wait! There has been so much commotion going on, that I forgot to tell you that Gal won't be able to make it. Something came up at work and she can't get away.", sighed Pink Rose.

"You know it doesn't surprise me with everything that is going on.", huffed Guy, "But I'm not going to allow any of it to discourage me. This is a special day for Beautiful and me."

Guy kissed his mother on the cheek and left her to finish preparations for the dinner. He realized that he hadn't heard from Cassie in two days and not talking frequently wasn't like them. He pulled out his cell phone and noticed it was still set to the silent setting. He had missed several calls and texts from Cassie, Pete, and Tim. Guy decided to call his pals on three-way and then address his fiancée afterward.

"Hey Pete, give me a moment to add Tim.", announced Guy.

"Sure ...", Pete uttered perplexed.

"Tim?", voiced Guy.

"Yeah.", Tim confirmed.

"Let me add Pete to the call.", Guy informed, "Pete are you here?"

"Sure am.", Pete said.

"Okay fellas, I didn't feel like discussing this shit twice so that's why I'm doing this three-way call.", Guy sighed.

"What's up? Is your ma, okay?", Pete questioned fearfully.

"Ma is fine, thank God. It's the farm; it was attacked again last night ...", Guy began.

"What the hell?", Pete fussed.

"Damn, another attack. How did you know the water was contaminated?", questioned Tim.

"How did you know about the attempted water contamination?", Guy inquired.

"Attempted? Well, you know word gets around fast and sometimes it's not always accurate.", chuckled Tim nervously.

"Yeah, it does. I heard about multiple scares on the premises, but I didn't know the details.", claimed Pete.

"The details are fucking unbelievable. We think an acquisition company is behind the attacks. I need to figure out a way to put an end to this shit. So, I'll be on hiatus for a minute. I need to focus on this acquisition company and my girl … and nothing else for a bit.", Guy advised.

"I get it, brother. Just reach out when you need to.", Pete offered.

"Oh, yeah; definitely do that.", Tim seconded.

"I appreciate that, fellas. Now I need to call my girl.", Guy informed.

"Okay, brother.", Pete said and then disconnected.

"Bye.", said Tim.

Guy disconnected and was perturbed that rumors were going around town and his friends had not said anything about it. He didn't want the community to start to believe that his family had lost their strength or resilience. That would only fuel the acquisition company's attempts and anyone else who thought they could come to town and try to push them out. The only people who had the power to push anyone out of Staton was the Staton family and he wanted to keep it that way.

Cassie was nervous, anxious, and frightened seemingly at once as she pondered why she hadn't heard from Guy. Her conscience told her that perhaps he had somehow put the puzzle pieces together and realized why she had come to town, she thought or maybe that bitch of a mother had convinced him that he would be better off with a little blond from down the road. Cassie sighed as her imagination ran wild then she stared at the beautiful dress she planned to wear. Just as Cassie began to moan like a lost schoolgirl, she heard Guy's ringtone from her cell phone. She jogged over to the nightstand to retrieve it.

"Hey Cowboy!", Cassie exclaimed.

"Hey! How are you, Beautiful?", asked Guy.

"I'm good. I was just wondering what was up with you.", confessed Cassie.

"Sorry, I accidentally left my phone on silent. So, I missed a shitload of calls yesterday.", Guy sighed.

Cassie knew something was off from his tone.

"What's going on? It's not like you to cuss with me.", Cassie explained.

"I'm sorry, Beautiful. I have a lot weighing on my mind, but I promise when I see you this evening, I won't focus on anything but you.", Guy vowed, "I'll send Mr. Henry for you in two hours."

"That's perfect, Cowboy. See you soon.", Cassie purred.

Cassie instantly realized it was not perfect; she wouldn't have a chance to talk until she arrived at his home.

"Fuck it!", Cassie blurted.

At that point, she had dodged or missed every opportunity to discuss her truth with Guy; so, she had resolved to allow the devil on her shoulder to be victorious. Cassie would boldly enter the Staton mansion as Guy's fiancée. Cassie would have one lasting victory over Pink Rose and gladly accept a loss in acquiring their company for her employer. Having a lifelong victory over Pink Rose and flaunting it over her would be victory enough, Cassie thought. She giggled as she imagined each passing holiday and the birth of their children; each event would be a knife in Pink Rose's back.

"Victory bitch!", laughed Cassie as she slid on her dress.

The angel on her other shoulder questioned her about Guy's reaction and cautioned her to be honest, but she silenced the voice.

"That man thinks I'm fine as fuck. I got him wrapped around my finger. He's not going anywhere.", Cassie smirked.

Cassie taunted fate with her comments and jiggled her breast in the mirror beneath the soft fabric of the dress. She looked even more stunning than the day she tried on the dress in the boutique. She wore her hair up in a messy bun; she allowed some ringlets to hang down to frame her face. She couldn't leave without making sure she had on her engagement ring and the beautiful pendant Guy had given her.

"Princess, what do you think, girl?", questioned Cassie.

Cassie twirled for Princess' inspection. Princess barked her approval and ran in circles chasing her tail. The excitement and positive energy bounced from Cassie to Princess and back again. The two were extremely excited about their futures. Mr. Henry pulled in front of the rental property and blew the horn. The horn distracted Princess causing her to bolt toward the front door. It was time to make her entrance, thought Cassie. Cassie exited the property and turned to see Mr. Henry opening the door of the Rolls Royce for her to enter.

"Hello, Ms. Cassie.", greeted Mr. Henry.

"Hello.", greeted Cassie.

Cassie entered the vehicle and inhaled deeply. The smell of the leather was intoxicating and it was a reminder of what Guy would afford her. It was a lifestyle she had desired her entire life and had worked so hard to obtain; it was oddly within her grasp after a simple business trip to a small town in Mississippi. The ride to the farm seemed much shorter than she knew it logistically was. Cassie's gaze went from her ring to the beautiful countryside as they neared Staton Farms and the family compound. It was breathtaking.

Mr. Henry pressed a hidden remote to open the white fence that closed off the property from the rest of the world. As the massive white gates opened, it seemed as if Cassie were entering a sacred world. A world that fostered and created the man with whom she had fallen in love. As the vehicle drove the winding road past barns, pastures, and office buildings, they approached the sprawling white mansion near a small pond. Cassie could hear the tires navigate the gravel ground and dirt road leading to the home. Each granule of soil on the compound represented Guy's lineage, power, and wealth; a lineage to which she would someday contribute.

Cassie looked out the window wide-eyed as she waited for Mr. Henry to open the door. She was astonished at the size and simple elegance of the massive white mansion. It was a two-story farmhouse mansion designed in an L-shape with rooms above the spacious four-car garage. The garage had doors on the front and rear; Cassie noticed that one stall had both doors open providing a view to the back of the property. There were two immense chimney stacks on the west wing of the home. She hoped one of them was connected to Guy's bedroom.

Guy entered the study off the main foyer.

"Ma, is everything ready?", questioned Guy nervously.

"Yes, there is no need to be nervous. I've been nervous enough for the two of us.", laughed Pink Rose, "I can't wait to meet her and give her this one-of-a-kind figurine I made for her."

Pink Rose smiled at her son and thought again of how wonderful it would have been for his father to witness that day.

"Your father would be so proud of you Guy.", smiled Pink Rose.

Guy hugged her quickly before he got too mushy.

"I think I heard the door open.", Guy informed, "Wait here, let me greet her first."

Henry entered and held the door open for Cassie to enter; her feet almost refused to cross the threshold as she knew everything would change forever.

"Right this way, Miss.", instructed Henry.

"I can take it from here, Mr. Henry!", beamed Guy.

"Yes indeed, sir.", smiled Henry.

Henry saw that Guy adored Cassie and his eyes were full of love and admiration.

"Beautiful ... I'm speechless.", Guy smiled as he twirled her into his arms.

He kissed her passionately and yearned to savor the few moments before taking her into the study to introduce her to his mother. He reluctantly pulled his lips from hers, yet he was desperate to kiss her more, so he kissed her shoulders and neck instead.

"Guy.", whispered Cassie in a giggle.

"All right, let me introduce you to my mother.", Guy whispered.

Cassie inhaled deeply as she followed him to the study. Pink Rose anticipated Guy and his fiancée; she stood beside the sofa not far from the entrance holding the beautiful glass figurine. Guy entered first with Cassie holding his hand following in tow.

"Ma, this is my beautiful fiancée, Cassandra Wiliams.", Guy announced.

Cassie sashayed boldly around the corner of the doorway and entered the room.

"I know the fuck she isn't!", shouted Pink Rose.

Pink Rose hurled the delicate figurine at Cassie, barely missing her as she dodged the beautiful gift that was turned into a weapon. It shattered as it hit one of the open double doors.

"Bitch, I don't know what kind of games you are playing ...", shouted Pink Rose.

"Ma, what is wrong with you? Don't yell at my fiancée.", warned Guy in his deeper register.

"No baby; it's okay.", assured Cassie, "Hello, Pink Rose, Ms. Rose, Pink, uh ... Mrs. Staton. Did I miss any of your aliases?"

"This is the bitch who is trying to get us to sell our family legacy.", Pink Rose accused.

"No, I am no longer on that assignment.", Cassie updated.

Guy was stunned and stared barely comprehending what he was hearing as he watched the beginnings of the catfight his mother had warned would happen.

"Bitch, you need to leave my house if you don't want me to kick your ass!", warned Pink before she lunged for Cassie.

Guy instantly came out of his daze to jump between the two women.

"Naw, let that bitch hit me.", laughed Cassie, "I've been holding back... before I had to check the bitch in me so I wouldn't have to slap a bitch. But now if she hits me ..."

Cassie shuffled backward and raised her hands to show all bets were off and she was ready to box with her future mother-in-law. At that point, everything was starting to sink in for Guy as his mind emerged from a shock-induced fog.

"Cassie, is what my mother said true? Did you come to town to scheme and force us to sell our family business?", asked a confused Guy, "Did you poison our cattle?"

"What? Scheme? I don't know what you're talking about.", confessed Cassie, "I just talked with your mother by phone and met in person once for my employer. This is my first time coming to the property. I could never do something so heartless!"

"You lying crook! You've done everything you could think of to hurt us including trying to poison our water supply.", accused Pink Rose, "But you are a true whore to use your body and manipulate my son into having a relationship with you just to win at this sick game you're playing."

"Wait a minute cow! Maybe that's the only way *you* can get what you want, but I don't have to sell my body bitch!", erupted Cassie, "I didn't know he was a Staton until after I had fallen in love with him, and even then, he didn't tell me he was KC Staton III."

The strong-willed women continued to hurl insults at one another as Guy replayed every scene with Cassie in his mind and thought of the discussions with and about the acquisition company. He felt a tight knot develop in his gut and his head began to pound with each beat of his broken heart.

"Enough!" growled Guy, "I don't want to hear another god-damned word from either of you! Cassie, you are not the woman I thought I fell in love with. I'm done. You need to leave. Mr. Henry!"

Henry hadn't gone far before everything erupted; he, like Cassie, had hoped everything could smooth itself out. After all, Cassie was every bit the type of woman Guy was drawn to; it would just take some time for him to forgive her, thought Henry as he entered the study.

"Yes, sir. What can I do for you?", inquired Henry.

"Remove this bitch …", shouted Pink.

"Ma!", shouted Guy, "Mr. Henry get Ms. Williams out of my sight. I don't care where you take her; you can drop her off on the side of the road somewhere. I don't give a fuck, just get her out of my house!"

"Guy, please you don't understand.", begged Cassie, "I haven't been on the case in weeks."

"Shut up, bitch! Mr. Fitzpatrick said he was following the plan you had put in place.", screamed Pink Rose, "Get this lying whore out of our home!"

Cassie wanted to grovel at Guy's feet, an act she had never done. However, she would have done anything at that moment to convince Guy to hear her out and accept that she had nothing to do with those horrific attacks. How could he even think she could do that for real; her eyes questioned Guy as tears filled them. She was momentarily immobilized hoping her tears could convince him to listen, but instead, his gaze grew cold, and then he turned his back to her.

"Come Ms. Cassie.", instructed Henry, and then he whispered, "It will work itself out, don't you worry."

Cassie felt faint; she had never been in love and therefore never experienced a broken heart. It was as though something had her lungs and heart in a chokehold. Her body was limp and Henry practically carried her from the mansion. She was blinded by tears, deaf from shock, and weakened by a broken heart. All she could hear was her conscience saying she should have confessed long ago. The next thing she remembered was Henry pulling in front of her rental home; she had fainted and awakened to a drenched dress wet from her tears.

Chapter 11

Cassie had a sleepless night and was dizzy from tears and a night of sobbing. Princess ran to her countless times to try to soothe her but to no avail. The only person, who could soothe her, refused to take her calls. Instead of attempting to reach Guy again, she called her Aunt Gloria, who seemed always to have the answer.

"Cassie, what's wrong?", asked Gloria.

Had Cassie been anyone else, Gloria would have assumed she had been crying.

"Auntie!", cried Cassie.

Cassie could barely breathe and Gloria was in shock and hesitated to respond.

"Baby girl?", questioned Gloria.

"I fucked up!", sobbed Cassie.

"What on earth did you do?", asked Gloria.

"I went to our engagement dinner without confessing anything to Guy and then that bitch …", cried Cassie, "She ruined everything! She threw a figurine at me and tried to attack me!"

"Baby girl, you know this is your fault, right?", advised Gloria.

"Huh?", sniffled Cassie.

"Yes. Had you been honest and upfront from the beginning, you probably wouldn't be crying right now.", informed Gloria.

"But … Auntie…", sniffled Cassie.

"Yes, baby. But if he really loves you, he will eventually hear you out. I don't know how long that will take.", explained Gloria, "Keep reaching out to him."

"He won't take my calls or text me back.", moaned Cassie, "I don't know what to do without him!"

"Well, that's why you won't stop. You are a very tenacious woman so you'll figure something out.", advised Gloria, "Have you eaten or got out of the house?"

"No ...", began Cassie.

"Get up! Eat, go for a run, do anything but lay around crying. Your tears won't change a thing; only action can do that!", insisted Gloria, "Remember who the hell you are!"

"Yes, Auntie.", whispered Cassie.

"Bye Baby Girl.", said Gloria.

"Okay bye.", whispered a weakened Cassie.

Cassie inhaled deeply as she stood and approached the mirror. She would take her aunt's advice and fight for her man. She wiped away her tears, pulled her hair back into a ponytail, and stood tall.

"You heard your Auntie. Remember who the fuck you are! You are Cassandra Denise Williams and you always get what the fuck you want, bitch!", Cassie brashly affirmed.

Cassie called for Princess and the two of them headed out for a late jog and she was determined to shower and eat upon her return. She loved Guy more than she knew was possible; she did not want to let go of the best man she had ever met. She vowed to God if He allowed her to win him back, there would be nothing she wouldn't do for Guy to keep him and make him proud to call her his wife.

173

The morning at the Staton mansion was not much different from the Airbnb. Pink Rose was worried about her son as she stood outside his bedroom listening; she had never seen him so angry. She had trouble sleeping and her difficulty was compounded by growls she heard coming from his bedroom. Even Boy ran from his room on more than one occasion when Guy threw objects against the walls. As much as she hated that Northern bitch, she hated even more admitting that Cassie was the best thing for her son. However, she felt she would declare defeat if she encouraged him to call Cassie. So, instead, she would be a quiet support for her son if he needed her.

Guy's head was pounding and he felt nauseated each time he ignored Cassie's calls or text messages. He desperately wanted to respond, but how could he forgive such a lie? He believed that her ability to lie to him proved they did not have a solid foundation for a marriage. Despite what his heart felt, his mind refused to consider accepting any communication from her. Half the day was gone and he continued to lay in his bed with red eyes from angry tears and his face flushed from rage. He was about to throw his glass bedside clock when Cassie called again. He hesitated but decided to answer even if it was only to cuss her out.

"What the hell do you want?", Guy's voice bellowed.

"Cowboy, please hear me out. You should know I had nothing at all to do with those attacks. I have grown to love Staton, the people, and everything about you. Why would you think I want to destroy our children's legacy?", implored Cassie.

"What else could I think when you were never honest about your connection?", insisted Guy.

Although her mention of children touched his heart and ignited his imagination, he couldn't hear past his doubts and his mother's warnings.

"Trust that I would never lie to you.   That's all I ask.", pleaded Cassie.

"Trust? You were not mindful of the consequences before you broke that trust. That was your first mistake.", whispered Guy.

Guy grew silent while on the call with Cassie.

"Guy?", questioned Cassie fearful that he had disconnected.

"Cassie, I'm done. Keep the ring as a warning of what not to do in your next relationship.", Guy disconnected the call.

"Guy!", screamed Cassie.

Cassie collapsed on the sofa into a fetal position and sobbed as if her world was ending. Princess came and licked her tears away but it was an endless stream of pain and regret. Princess realized her actions were pointless so she climbed on the sofa and snuggled close to Cassie and Cassie buried her face deep within the fur of her precious girl.

Gloria did not like to butt into her niece's love life, but she realized this relationship was far different from those of the past, and a different approach was needed.

"Gina. Your daughter messed up.", informed Gloria.

"Oh goodness. Do you mean she didn't tell Guy the truth?", Gina inquired.

"Sure, the hell did not!", fussed Gloria.

"Oh, Lord.", whispered Gina.

"I don't like to be in folks' business, but I thought you should know. Okay, I'll talk later.", informed Gloria.

"Okay, talk later.", Gina said.

"What was that about? Is Cassie in trouble down there in Mississippi?", worried Cassie's father, Mitch.

"Well, sweetie ...", Gina began.

Anyone connected to the town or the acquisitions company was in flux about the attacks on Staton Farms and the rumors. The conspirator decided to call Fitzpatrick so the two could develop another scheme and attack Guy during his weakened stage.

"Look Fitzpatrick, I have another idea for a guaranteed victory.", boasted the conspirator.

"Listen, things have gotten out of control and I don't need the heat. I don't know about you but I need to keep my job. So, I've decided to accept defeat and move on to other equally big fish.", Fitzpatrick asserted.

"Wait a god-damn minute!", insisted the conspirator.

"Buddy, you're on your own!", ordered Fitzpatrick before hanging up.

"Fuck!", shouted the conspirator in his office, "I'm too close to breaking Guy to stop now."

He banged his fists on his rich mahogany desk as he vowed to break the powerful family once and for all; no matter how he had to do it. He knew the ends and outs of the farm well and he had known the Staton family all his life, so he didn't need RQ Acquisitions for anything. He would avenge his family and his childhood broken heart by making the family pay for what they had done to his parents.

Time and life moved along after Cassie's and Guy's worlds had imploded, but the couple's capacity to push through was intangible. Cassie was depressed and sulked around for at least two weeks after Guy called off the wedding. Time didn't flow the same since then and she wasn't sure how many days or weeks it had been. The only thing she was sure of, was that she no longer wanted to work for RQ Acquisitions; there was no way she could work for a company that would back the attacks that occurred. In addition to searching for an airline ticket, she also had applied to several companies in New York; perhaps it was time for her to return to the freedom a life in New York provided. She was done begging Guy and felt that her endless messages were starting to make her look desperate instead of the heartbroken love of his life. Princess behaved like an empath, she would mope around the rental and sleep most of the day. Cassie felt guilty when she noticed how her sorrow had impacted her sweet girl.

"Princess!", called Cassie.

Princess came eagerly running toward her best friend. It had been too long since Cassie had given her any attention.

"I'm sorry girl. I know I haven't paid attention to you, but that will change. We are getting out of this house, going into town, and then for a run.", promised Cassie.

Princess seemed to understand every word as she jumped onto Cassie's lap as she sat at the dining room table. Princess could not contain her joy and licked Cassie's face nonstop. Princess was not the only pet empath; Boy was frantic and walked in circles mimicking Guy as he paced his office floor. Guy hated that Cassie's text messages and calls had stopped, but he wasn't sure he wanted to contact her. His heart had softened toward her and was perhaps ready to hear her out, but he was slightly stubborn and wanted to remain detached from her.

His detachment from the love of his life could be seen and felt whenever he engaged with family, friends, or employees; it caused him to be short-tempered and irritated about things that normally didn't bother him. He was disillusioned and fooled only himself if he thought he could live without Cassie. Henry stepped by Guy's office; he had decided that he had remained quiet long enough.

"Mr. Staton?", questioned Henry.

"Yes, Mr. Henry.", acknowledged Guy.

"May I speak to you, sir?", asked Henry.

"Of course, any time. Come in.", reassured Guy.

Henry began speaking as he entered the room.

"Although I've worked for this family a very long time, I have always stayed in my lane and focused on the work of a head butler.", Henry paused.

"Yes, you have ... please continue Mr. Henry.", insisted Guy.

"Sir, your and your father's personality traits are identical. You share many of the same loves that your father did, including loving headstrong and independent women. I could go on, but I'll sum it up by saying that Ms. Cassie is everything you love in a woman. Ms. Cassie and Ms. Pink Rose are cut from the same cloth. They are determined women with a heart of gold hidden and tucked away. They don't show their vulnerability to everyone.", Henry paused again.

"Your point?", inquired Guy.

"That you would be, forgive my bluntness, a fool not to take her back. Women like them are hard to find and to love, but once they let you in to experience their love; it's unmatched!", laughed Henry, "I have one of my own so I know what I'm talking about."

Guy was shocked that Henry would speak so boldly, but Henry gave him food for thought. They were thoughts that he had already been thinking yet, he was unsure if he should act upon them. Guy's gaze turned to Henry as a little boy pleased to receive encouragement from someone he admired. Guy nodded at Henry as a form of dismissal and thankfulness. Henry smiled at Guy knowing that his words had reached Guy's heart. Guy's eyes showed he admitted he loved her too much to let her leave his life.

"Boy!", called Guy.

Boy came running; he was excited that his best pal called his name with life infused in his voice. He jumped on Guy's leg and waited for a pat and affection. Guy rubbed Boy's head as he talked.

"Mr. Henry is right. I'm being a damn fool. I can't lose Beautiful. Let's go get my girl back!", laughed Guy.

I don't know why the fuck she would want to come to this little hick town, thought Jaquan as the Lift driver drove through the wooden areas and around the country-curved roads. He hoped he would convince her to leave the backwoods and return to Detroit with him. The vehicle pulled in front of the Airbnb to drop off Jaquan. He barely acknowledged the driver when he tossed an extra tip to the front passenger seat and then gathered his duffle bag to exit the car.

"A little something extra.", bragged Jaquan.

He was feeling good about his latest business venture and that the father of the hottest bitch he knew was supporting him. He rang the doorbell and knocked, but there was no answer. So, he assumed Cassie had gone out for a run since her rental car was still parked outside. Jaquan decided to call Mitch to provide an update.

"Thanks for giving me the passcode. It looks like Cassie isn't here right now.", informed Jaquan.

"I'm glad she gave it to us for emergency purposes. Make sure my daughter is okay. I don't know what the hell that white boy did to her.", fussed Mitch.

"You know I got my girl's back! I should never have let her get away!", insisted Jaquan.

"Well, you're back now and it's the perfect time to earn her trust.", advised Mitch.

"Thanks, that's why you that motherfucker!", laughed Jaquan, "Let me holla at you later; this heat is a bitch! I'm going inside to wait for my girl."

Guy was nervous despite driving that road a dozen times that led to Cassie's place. He just hoped he wasn't too late and she would take him back. Boy road shotgun and licked Guy's face to reassure him that things would work out. He had allowed Boy's influence to inspire hope as he pulled onto the property and parked his truck. Guy rolled the windows down.

"Stay here, boy.", ordered Guy.

Jaquan heard a vehicle parked next to Cassie's car; he was curious to see who was stopping by. He thought it was a little late in the day for a maid to stop by; maybe it was a chef, he hoped. He tossed his duffle bag on the sofa and returned to the door to answer the doorbell. Guy didn't hear Princess barking inside but someone was there as he heard heavy steps nearing the door. Jaquan opened the door to discover Guy and assumed that the property management must have sent a handyman.

"What are you here to fix?", questioned Jaquan.

"Pardon?", asked a confused Guy.

Jaquan sized Guy up and realized he was no repairman after he gazed around to see the expensive truck parked alongside Cassie's vehicle. Instead, he was the white man who had broken Cassie's heart, but he wasn't the frail specimen Jaquan had expected.

"Who the hell are you?", demanded Guy.

"I ask the questions motherfucka. You came to *my* bitch's place.", fumed Jaquan.

Guy attempted to push past Jaquan believing that Cassie might be in trouble. There was no way that she would date a thug like the man blocking the doorway.

"I need to speak to my fiancée!", insisted Guy.

Guy tried to look around for signs of Cassie, Princess, or a struggle, but Jaquan's body mass matched his own making it difficult to see into the house.

"I don't know who the fuck you are, but if you don't let me inside you are going to have a problem.", warned Guy.

"You don't need to know who the fuck I am. Just know Cassie is my bitch and that ass belongs to me.", shouted Jaquan as he bucked forward and put his finger in Guy's face.

"I wouldn't advise you to do that.", Guy uttered calmly.

Jaquan chuckled; he thought it was humorous for any country white boy to believe he could do anything with him. And what Jaquan couldn't do, his handgun, tucked in his waistband, most definitely would do the rest.

"And what will you do if I don't?', instigated Jaquan.

Jaquan pointed his finger in Guy's face again, this time touching his nose; he didn't get the response he expected. Guy smirked at the arrogance of the tall stranger before he grabbed his finger breaking the bone. Jaquan growled in pain as Guy took full control of the situation and Jaquan's body as he twisted the limb with the broken digit to Jaquan's back. Guy then removed the handgun and kicked Jaquan on the back sending him off the porch onto a bed of rose bushes. Guy in one quick motion dislodged the bullet chamber from the handgun rendering the weapon useless and tossed the objects in different directions.

"I got something for you bitch!", shouted Jaquan.

Jaquan struggled to get to his feet as he felt for his handgun. He was shocked that it was no longer there. He stumbled before falling a second time on another rose bush face first. Boy barked frantically from the driver seat as he fought the urge to spring from the window and defend his best pal.

"If Cassie would rather be with you then I don't stand a chance even if I beat your ass.", conceded Guy.

Guy marched to his truck, pushed Boy to the passenger seat, and sped off as soon as he cranked the engine. Guy couldn't believe Cassie would rush to the arms of an apparent loser like that thug; he realized he didn't even know the man's name, but did it really matter? Guy decided it did not as he spotted Cassie and Princess approaching the house. Cassie looked furious, but he couldn't tell if those feelings were aimed at him or the stranger whimpering from the broken forefinger and rose thorns. Boy and Princess barked their greetings from afar not understanding why their best pals wouldn't make up.

Cassie stood still as her eyes followed Guy's truck down the driveway. She barely believed that he had finally come for her only to encounter the fool standing on the landing holding his hand crying like a bitch, she thought.

"Jaquan, what the fuck are you doing here and how did my door get opened?", shouted Cassie.

Cassie stormed toward him pointing to her opened door.

"Your father sent me here to check on you and gave me the code," Jaquan partially lied.

Princess hated Jaquan and growled ferociously.

"Calm down girl. I might let you bite into that ass later.", instructed Cassie.

Princess quieted down and licked her lips as if savoring the opportunity.

"My father knows better. He taught me to kick ass. So, why are you really here?", demanded Cassie.

Cassie walked to the landing and got a better look at Jaquan; she saw he had an injured finger, scratches on his face, and a torn shirt from his multiple falls.

"Looks like Guy beat that ass.", smirked Cassie.

"Naw, that bitch almost got beat. He tripped me when I tried to throw the first punch.", lied Jaquan, "I better never see his bitch ass again or I'll fuck him up on-site, 'cause I defend mines."

"Jaquan, I *never* was yours.", corrected Cassie, "In case you didn't know, I was just community pussy and you were community dick. When I needed some dick, I called you. When I wanted to go out, I called you. When I wanted my pussy ate out, I called you. Did I *call* you?", sputtered Cassie.

Jaquan was shocked and silenced by her words.

"No, I did not. So why the fuck are you here?", whispered Cassie.

Jaquan quickly got over the shock of Cassie's revelation and responded.

"I want us to get back what we had ...", paused an embarrassed Jaquan, "but my calls go to your voicemail."

"That's because I'm done with yo' ass.", Cassie informed.

"Girl, don't be like that!", begged Jaquan.

Cassie walked inside the house and Princess followed, but she walked backward as she growled at Jaquan. Cassie noticed his duffle bag on the sofa and picked it up. She tossed it to Jaquan who hurt his finger more when he attempted to catch it.

"Take your shit and leave!", demanded Cassie.

"Cassie ...", began Jaquan.

"I guess you want Princess to bite that ass.", smirked Cassie.

Jaquan did not leave but inched closer to Cassie instead.

"Princess, he's all yours, girl.", promised Cassie.

Princess growled showing her teeth and immediately charged for Jaquan who had to put his long legs to use like he did in his college days running yards for Wayne State University. However, running on gravel was not as easy as running on grass. He lost his footing several times as Princess chased him down the driveway. Cassie whistled for Princess to return leaving Jaquan at the side of the road to call for a ride.

Any other time Cassie would have laughed hysterically at the sight of Princess chasing Jaquan, but all she could think about was her time in Mississippi was coming to a head. She and Princess were scheduled to leave on an early flight the next morning. She desperately wanted to call Guy; however, she had called and texted enough for the two, since their failed engagement dinner. This time it was up to him to call her since his first attempt at winning her back was ruined by Jaquan. Guy owed her at least that much, she thought. Yet, Cassie wasn't sure if her stubbornness had her believing that or if it was a reasonable request. Regardless, she wasn't doing anything remotely related to KC Guy Staton III.

"Come on girl, let's get packed.", Cassie instructed as she and Princess entered the house.

Chapter 12

Cassie had been settled back home for a couple of weeks, but every day she thought she would open her condominium door to find Guy with a bouquet of roses asking her to return. Instead, nothing, not even a call from the man with whom she was hopelessly in love. Michelle had insisted that they hang out and she had made up excuse after excuse to turn down Michelle's invitations. However, Cassie knew that if she wanted to settle back into her pre-Guy life she needed to get back out there with Michelle and do the things she enjoyed doing. So, there she was waiting at the table for a late Michelle to arrive as usual; at least she could count on Michelle to be Michelle if nothing else.

Cassie spotted a sassy Michelle entering the new trendy downtown Detroit restaurant. The restaurant was one of many that sprung up as young professionals moved downtown to experience a hip and fun lifestyle. Cassie was feeling uneasy about her decision to come; she could see from the piercing eyes of several men that it would be quite easy to get back into the dating scene. However, she wasn't sure if she was ready for that. Michelle on the other hand was ready for the dating scene; she wore cream leather leggings with a one-shoulder cream Luis Vuitton knit pullover. Michelle's gold bangle bracelets, hoop earrings, and gold stiletto sandals drew far more attention than Cassie's blue jeans and grey off-the-shoulder sweatshirt with sneakers.

"Hey, Cassie!", greeted Michelle as she leaned down to hug her, "You look different."

"Uh, thanks, I guess.", chuckled Cassie.

"I can't put my finger on it.", Michelle pondered then noticed the engagement ring, "That's what it is."

Michelle pointed to the exquisite diamond engagement ring on Cassie's slender finger.

"What?", questioned Cassie.

"Why are you still wearing his ring and dressed like you don't give a fuck about getting a new man?", pried Michelle.

"To be honest, I don't want a new man. I want Guy.", moaned Cassie.

"Well... I hate to break it to you, but you don't have him. And if he gave two fucks, he would be here.", Michelle advised.

"That's not true. I'm the one who fucked up, remember?", Cassie corrected.

"Regardless of who is to blame, the outcome is the same. You are alone.", whispered Michelle, "And the best way to get over one man is to have another man on top of you."

Cassie shook her head in disagreement and sighed.

"I don't feel that way anymore. I think the best thing for me to do now is focus on my new job and then decide what I want out of life. I believed I wanted to move back to New York, but ...", sighed Cassie, "Country living really changed everything for me."

Cassie noticed that Michelle barely heard anything she had said. The bad boy at the table across from them had captured Michelle's attention and mind. There was no point in Cassie continuing to share her thoughts with her best friend; instead, she signaled the waiter to come. The waiter nodded and then stopped by the bad boy's table first.

"Mr. Bianchi, do you need anything else?", inquired the waiter.

"It's just, Giovanni," Giovanni said with his eyes fixed on Michelle, then moved his attention to the waiter. "No, I don't. Just bring the check and add theirs to my tab. Thanks."

The waiter's eyes followed the direction of Giovanni's gaze and nodded.

"Are you having dinner with me or the douche over there?", sneered Cassie.

"Sorry, *I'm* still in the dating game.", laughed Michelle, "And that one looks like money and *I* don't pass up guys with money like you do."

"Shut up, bitch.", laughed Cassie, "Let's order."

Chip and some other crew members were uneasy that Guy had not been himself for the last month. They found themselves taking on his farm responsibilities and Pink took on more decisions from the Farm operations office. She had tried to give him time to grieve, but he had been taking far longer than she believed necessary, especially with the looming threat of RQ Acquisitions. She had no idea when or if another attack or tactic would show itself. She wanted to assert herself and tell him to get his act together and do something about the situation; however, she had no idea how he would take her interference. However, she could no longer remain silent; so, she reluctantly entered his home office. She found him sitting at his desk and his eyes looked like they were a lifetime away.

"Guy.", Pink began.

"Yes, Ma.", sighed Guy then covered his mouth with his hands in contemplation.

"I didn't want to put in my two cents, but I think it's time for you to fly to Detroit and convince Cassie to come home with you."

Guy looked up with questioning eyes; he wasn't sure he heard his mother correctly.

"Guy, are you listening to me?", Pink asked sternly.

"Yeah … you want me to do what?", asked Guy.

187

"You heard me. Go to her!", ordered Pink, "She's no different than me. Before I married your father, I used to argue all the time with your grandma Staton.",

Guy perked up and sat attentively as his mother continued.

"Really?", questioned Guy.

He had never heard any of those stories growing up.

"You two seemed to get along well. You even spoke at her funeral.", Guy said with a confused expression.

"We did get along once your father and I married. That's when I realized that she had only been trying to protect her favorite.", laughed Pink, "Your father was such a momma's boy."

"This sounds so familiar.", chuckled Guy.

"I'm serious. Cassie is good for you.", confessed Pink, "All I've ever wanted is for you to be happy and she does that for you."

"I ...", Guy struggled to speak.

Pink walked over to her son to lean down and hug him as she rested her head atop his.

"I can't tell you what to do, but I am telling you that you need to do something.", Pink whispered before kissing his forehead.

Guy watched his mother walk away and leave the office. Her words shocked him; he would never have imagined that she of all people would support him being with Cassie. He pinched himself to confirm that he was awake and not dreaming. He laughed as the idea crossed his mind that his mother only wanted to ensure a thriving business and if that meant enduring Cassie so be it; it would be a small price for her to pay. Regardless of her reasons, she supported their union and her support meant everything to Guy. Now it was up to him to decide if he would return to the land of the living.

Guy's friends had invited him to join them for a night out. Tim had suggested Silverbacks, but Trixy did not want to hang out at her workplace on her night off and she said she wouldn't join them unless they decided on a different location. So, Guy sent a group text and made a last-minute suggestion by inviting them to his home. He was pleased that they agreed; it would be good to hang out with them again. They hadn't done so since he introduced Cassie to them, and that seemed like a lifetime ago, thought Guy. He called Henry's cell phone to set things up for the evening.

"Hey, Mr. Henry.", Guy greeted.

"Hello, Mr. Staton. What can I do for you?", inquired Henry.

"I'm inviting the guys and Trixy over this evening for cards. I'll need things prepared.", Guy informed.

"Of course, sir.", promised Henry.

One small step for Guy and one giant leap for Staton Farms, smiled Henry who was pleased that Guy was back to socializing with his friends. Guy felt the same way but feeling normal could only mean that Cassie was back in his life. He picked up his cell phone again and stared at her number. He desperately wanted to call her yet he questioned whether she even thought about him. Guy didn't know, but Cassie thought of him constantly; even as she attempted to eat the delicious lunch she had ordered.

"Hello.", Michelle said sarcastically.

Cassie looked up from her plate with confused eyes.

"So, are you going to play with it, eat it, or at least talk to me?", Michelle asked.

"I'm sorry. I can't stop thinking about Guy.", moaned Cassie.

"Why don't you call Jaquan for a good fuck, with his sexy black ass. That should take your mind off Guy.", advised Michelle.

189

"Girl, no. Like I said that's how the old me used to get down. Besides, I don't need you bringing up that loser. I'm still furious with Jaquan for tracking me down and a little pissed with my dad for giving him my information.", fussed Cassie.

"I still can't believe Poppa Mitch would do that.", Michelle giggled.

"That's because he doesn't realize that Jaquan is a hustler. My dad thinks Jaquan is a real businessman; instead of a master of the ghetto.", laughed Cassie.

"That's right! He said that he mastered the ghetto.", Michelle laughed, "Who says shit like that?"

"Exactly. He knows every trick or scheme to get ahead.", Cassie said in disapproval, "And that's not the type of man I want."

"I hear you. Like one old bird says, 'You gots to be more careful!'", laughed Michelle.

"Old bird...", laughed Cassie, "How is your grandmother doing?"

"Getting on my nerves. She keeps asking me when I'm going to get married and make her a great-grandmother.", laughed Michelle.

The two ladies were laughing and about to dive into their favorite old bird stories when Cassie's phone began to ring.

"Oh my God, it's Guy.", Cassie announced as she stared at the phone.

"Answer it!", Michelle insisted.

Cassie picked up the phone and stared at the picture she had saved as his contact. He was the most stunning man she had ever seen. As much as she wanted to answer, she was immobilized with fear. Fear of what she did not know. The two women stared at the phone until it stopped ringing and the call went to voicemail.

Cassie laid the phone on the table and then resumed nibbling on her food as if she had not received the most important call of her life.

"Are you going to check for a voicemail?", asked Michelle.

"He left one.", informed Cassie as she continued to eat.

"Okay ... well play it.", Michelle instructed.

"No ... I can't ... I don't want to hear his voice right now.", Cassie partially admitted the truth.

Truthfully, she did not know what to expect; he might have been calling to have his final words with her and tell her that she was a lowlife. Her heart was too weak to hear him berate her. When or if she listened to the message, it would be in the privacy of her own home.

"Why not?", asked Michelle.

"Let's drop it and talk about something else. So, what do you like about the douchebag at the other table?", Cassie diverted.

Michelle reluctantly gushed over the sexy Italian at the other table as she discretely texted Cassie's aunt and asked her to check on Cassie later. She didn't recognize the woman sharing a meal with her and did not know how to advise this *new* Cassie. Cassie feigned interest as Michelle lusted over the Italian and she nodded and smiled when appropriate, but her mind was in Mississippi where her heart remained.

It had been hours since Guy left the message for Cassie and he had not heard anything from her. Despite that, he hoped that he eventually would; if not, he would not allow that to deter him from his next plans. Plan two, was to enjoy his time with his friends when they arrived and he had already put plan one into motion when he made a call directly after leaving the message for Cassie. He contemplated his next moves as he stood looking at the glass of bourbon in his hand.

"Pour a glass for me!", teased Pete.

"Bro, what's wrong with your hands!", joked Guy, "It's good to see you guys!"

Tim and Trixy followed Pete inside the study and Guy greeted them with hugs.

"Help yourselves!", Guy instructed.

"I don't want any of that fancy shit. A beer will work for me.", laughed Trixy as she walked to the console serving as a bar.

"Whatever you want I'll make sure you get it.", laughed Guy as he pointed to the beers on ice.

"Man, it's good to see you rebounding. Brother, shit really has been hitting the fan for Staton Farms.", Pete acknowledged.

"Yeah, and it's probably not over.", informed Tim.

"What are you guys talking about?", Trixy asked, "I guess I'm out of the loop."

"Sorry, Trix, that I didn't tell you. It was too infuriating to talk about it.", Guy apologized.

"We heard more about it from townspeople than from Guy.", Pete explained.

"That's right. I forgot men are the biggest gossipers ever!", laughed Trixy, "You can fill me in later about that. So, how's our girl Cassie?"

"Damn, you are really out of the loop!", laughed Tim.

"Shit. What happened?", asked Trixy.

Pete and Tim filled her in on the news as if Guy was not in the room. Guy noticed how much Tim was getting a kick from telling the sad tale and was more animated than usual. Guy was becoming irritated by hearing the story as a bystander.

"She's a liar and a ruthless woman. I'm glad she's gone.", voiced Tim.

"Is she really though?", questioned Trixy.

"Please, let's move on to something else.", Guy directed.

"Yeah, moving on is exactly what you should do.", Tim advised, "You should never look back."

"Maybe, you did dodge a bullet.", suggested Pete.

"Guys!", Guy barked.

Pink was about to enter the study but paused in the hall to listen to the ill-advised advice of his peers. She wanted to storm inside the study and chastise Guy's friends by telling them to mind their business, but Henry requested her attention.

"Ms. Pink Rose, RQ Acquisitions is on the phone for you.", Henry informed.

Pink was disturbed and curious why a company representative would call that late. She was not in the mood for any of their schemes.

"I'll take the call in my office.", Pink advised.

Pink walked briskly to her office and inhaled deeply before answering.

"What the hell do you want?", demanded Pink.

"We are ending negotiations because we discovered someone, not affiliated with our company, engineered attacks on your farm.", Fitzpatrick explained, "That's not how we do business and we don't want to be associated with that."

"Do you have any idea who did it", Pink questioned.

"No, I just know none of my people would stoop so low.", advocated Fitzpatrick and then disconnected.

Pink held the phone to her heart as she prayed that this news meant it was an end to any more attacks. However, if the person behind the attacks did not work for Fitzpatrick, what would stop them from attacking again? Nevertheless, she would tell Guy that they no longer had to worry about RQ Acquisitions breathing down their necks and hopefully that chapter of their lives had ended.

Knowing that he had the full support of his mother and resolving in his mind to want Cassie in his life, afforded him a restful night and energized him to jump-start his day. Guy had awoke feeling refreshed; it had been weeks since he had slept soundly. He knew it was partially from spending time with his friends; however, he gave most of the credit to his feelings. And those feelings fueled his actions and the plan he had already set in motion. There was only one thing left to do so he would have all the information he needed. Guy contemplated his actions and what he needed to do to solidify his plans as he removed his cell phone from his office desk and made a call.

"Mr. Fitzpatrick, you have a call.", informed the secretary.

"Who is it? I don't have time to waste; I have a deadline to meet.", snarled Fitzpatrick.

"It's Mr. KC Staton of Staton Farms.", the secretary uttered.

"Transfer the call.", Fitzpatrick's voice quivered.

After last evening, Fitzpatrick thought he was finished with the fiasco and would never hear the name Staton again. What could he possibly want, thought Fitzpatrick.

"Hello. What can I do for you?", asked a hesitant Fitzpatrick.

"I need the address of one of your employees.", Guy informed.

"Sir, I am not allowed to do that.", chuckled Fitzpatrick, "I'm sure I would be breaking some HR policies if I did."

"I'm sure you've broken more than some HR policies in your time.", Guy accused, "And after what you put my family through, you owe me at least that much."

"Okay. Who is the employee?", questioned Fitzpatrick.

"Ms. Cassie Williams, my fiancée.", Guy disclosed.

No wonder she wanted him to remove her from the deal, thought Fitzpatrick.

"Look, we only have a mailing address for Ms. Williams.", Fitzpatrick informed.

"I'll take it and go from there.", insisted Guy.

"It's 55 Blue Jay's Nest in Detroit.", provided Fitzpatrick.

Guy thought it was an odd address, but Fitzpatrick reassured him before ending the call that it was legit and she received every piece of mail the company had sent there. So, Guy took the information and hopefully, the deceitful boss had not lied to him. Guy spotted Henry walking by his office door.

"Mr. Henry!", called Guy.

Henry doubled back to the office, glad to be of service to the young man he had come to love.

"Yes, Mr. Staton. How may I assist?", offered Henry.

"Well Mr. Henry ... I'm going to Detroit to win back my girl.", announced Guy.

"A great decision sir.", beamed Henry, "I assume you will take a company jet for an overnight stay?"

"Yes, I'll need you to arrange that for the soonest possible departure date. I'll also need limo service.", Guy detailed.

"What about hotel accommodations?", asked Henry.

"I hadn't thought about that.", sighed Guy, "I hope I won't need them."

"Yes of course, but I will have them arranged just in case.", informed Henry.

"Appreciate it.", Guy said pensively.

Staying alone in a hotel room or coming home alone was not an option. Guy had not considered any outcome other than him making love to Cassie in her bed or carrying her aboard the plane to make passionate love there. Guy leaned back in his office chair and closed his eyes; he could already feel Cassie in his arms and smell the scent of her hair and skin. He desired her touch, fragrance, and presence; it was too much for his mind and he could not control his body's reaction as his manhood strained against his zipper. Henry's return to the office shut down those thoughts before he had decided to do something inappropriate.

"Mr. Staton, as I research matters, I would suggest you fly into Coleman A. Young Municipal Airport within the Detroit city limits. It will be less hectic with fewer obstacles to delay your visit to Ms. Cassie. However, you will need to take the smaller jet for this trip. I will schedule the Stratos jet; it has a short take-off capacity.", Henry informed.

"I trust you know what's best. You can set it up.", Guy assured.

"Sir, I've already done so for tomorrow. The jet will leave at 11 am and I will personally chauffeur you to Staton Airport.", smiled Henry.

"Well ... I guess I'd better start packing.", Guy paused, "I'll need flowers ..."

"Mr. Staton ... have I ever let you down?", questioned Henry.

196

Guy chuckled.

"No.   Your limo will have everything you need for a romantic date … roses, champagne, fruits, and cheeses. Just make sure you look deserving of such an incredible woman.", teased Henry.

"I promise I'll do my best.", laughed Guy.

Chapter 13

Cassie was frustrated beyond words at herself, Fitzpatrick, Guy, and Pink; anybody in her life for the last several months. She blamed them all for her predicament and to make matters worse; she was not on top of her game and felt she was letting her new employer down. Despite her new boss being over the moon with her performance, she knew it did not represent what she was fully capable of doing. Her focus wasn't on her work, but memories of Guy and the dreams they shared for building a life together. Nothing in her world seemed to be on the right trajectory; not only was her performance low, she felt exhausted from doing nothing at all and was bitchier than usual. It was even more reason for her to be thankful that she worked remotely from home. Just as Cassie regained her focus on her work assignment, she received a call from Gloria.

"Really, Auntie?", sighed Cassie as she answered the call, "Hey, Auntie. What's up?"

"Nothing but checking on my fabulous niece.", informed Gloria.

"Let me guess, Mommy or Michelle begged you to check on me.", Cassie accused.

"I don't need a reason to check on you. But yes, Michelle was concerned.", paused Gloria, "So, have you heard from the young man?"

"No, Auntie, and please drop the subject. It hurts too much to talk about Guy.", Cassie pleaded.

"Doll, I think that you should step away from your work and swing by your parents' house this afternoon. It will be good for you to let us dote on you.", insisted Gloria, "I convinced your daddy to fry up some catfish and pull out the playing cards, but we can focus on you instead."

"That does sound like a good idea.", sighed Cassie, "I have to admit I haven't spent much time with any of you since I returned home."

Home thought Cassie, it was such an empty word when she used it to describe her place and city. The small towns of Raymond and Staton had felt more like home than any place had in her adult years. The friends she had made, Jill and Trixy, created a cozy environment and Guy made everything in between feel right. Gloria reacted to Cassie's silence that she was sure had to be filled with thoughts of Guy.

"Doll, I know you miss him terribly and that's to be expected. It will take some time for things to return to normal.", voiced Gloria.

"But that's the thing, Auntie. I don't know that I want things to return to *normal*.", Cassie breathed heavily.

The Rolls Royce pulled up to the private plane to send Guy on his way to Detroit. Henry exited the car to open the door for Guy only to find that Guy had already exited the vehicle. Henry changed his focus to removing Guy's bag from the trunk.

"Sir, I'll see you and Ms. Cassie soon when you two return home.", Henry prophesied.

"God, I hope so Mr. Henry. I hope so.", sighed Guy.

Guy retrieved his bag from Henry and began the ascent up the stairs leading to his private plane. In a few short hours, he would stand before his fiancée and reclaim her; his misery and loneliness would all be gone once he held her in his arms. After settling in his seat, he rested his head on the headrest and thought about her sweetness as he prepared for take-off. He braced himself as the plane sped on the track preparing for take-off. It was his first trip to Detroit and would undoubtedly be a memorable one. He had flown hundreds of times before; however, that morning he viewed the vastness of the sky as if for the first time and marveled at its beauty. He found peace, reassurance, and hope in the skies. Soon sleep enveloped Guy and he rested as he flew to Cassie's arms.

"Hey, Gina.", Gloria greeted her sister on the phone, "I convinced Cassie to come over to your place this afternoon."

"I'm surprised you got her to agree.", confessed Gina, "Her daddy and I have been asking her non-stop."

"Well, you know I can usually convince her to do whatever.", laughed Gloria.

"Yes, you can. You're lucky we aren't jealous about that.", teased Gina, "So no cards?"

"I told her to come by an hour after I arrive so that we can get in at least a couple of games.", Gloria informed.

"Okay, good because Mitch has been itching to beat you in at least one hand.", giggled Gina.

"He can try and that's about all he'll do.", laughed Gloria.

"Girl! Exactly. He is a horrible Spades player.", laughed Gina, "Okay, we'll see you soon."

"Yup, I'm heading out now. See you in a bit.", Gloria informed.

Guy awakened refreshed as the plane descended on the airstrip for the landing. Just as promised, Henry had a chauffeur service waiting for Guy as he deplaned. Inside the limousine, there were multiple bouquets of roses as promised. As he entered the vehicle, he spotted a florist truck nearing the plane and it stopped in front of the portable staircase. The driver and an assistant exited and began transporting more bouquets to the plane. Guy smiled as he thought of Henry's attention to detail, yet that same detail would be torture while flying home, if he were alone.

Gloria arrived at her sister's home earlier than planned; she wanted to ensure she and Cassie's parents had time to discuss her in case Cassie popped in before expected. She was about to ring the doorbell when Gina opened the door.

"Hey girl, I heard your car pull up.", laughed Gina.

"Don't even try it.", laughed Gloria.

"Mitch and I keep telling you to get those brakes checked.", teased Gina.

"Move", Gloria playfully teased, "I'm getting every bit of life out of those expensive brake pads."

"Keep it up and you'll mess up your rotors.", warned Mitchell as he greeted Gloria with a hug.

"Yeah, yeah, I think all of this talk is to put off a good butt whooping in Spades.", laughed Gloria, "Where are the cards?"

"I'll go get them.", laughed Mitchell.

Gloria walked to the sofa and plopped down as if the weight of the world were on her shoulders.

"You need to talk to Cassie ...", began Gloria.

"About what?", questioned Gina.

"About what? Guy of course. She needs to beg for his forgiveness because she was dead wrong for what she did and it's costing her a good man.", insisted Gloria.

"You know as well as I do my daughter is stubborn and won't listen to a soul if her mind is made up!", declared Gina, "And I'm not going to stress myself out because I already have a good man. That's up to her."

"Well, I don't and I didn't.", laughed Gloria, "So, I guess it's my battle to get through to her."

"Girl, that is not what I meant; but hell, if you want to fight that battle, who am I to stop you?", chuckled Gina.

Mitchell returned to the living room with the playing cards after hearing the tail end of the ladies' discussion.

"Well, I'm rooting for Jaquan to get her back.", blurted Mitchell.

The women scoffed at the idea.

"You sound crazy!", Gina scolded.

"Jaquan is doing well for himself.", informed Mitchell.

The women laughed at Mitchell's proclamation.

"It's nothing but smoke screens and mirrors.", declared Gina.

"That's right. He's a hustler and a liar.", Gloria claimed.

"He's never broke and won't ever be if he's a hustler.", Mitchell claimed.

"I think you, low-key wish you were like Jaquan or had been back in the day.", Gina accused.

"Nonsense.", Mitchell retorted.

Guy exited the limo with a bouquet of roses; he stood momentarily on the sidewalk as he inhaled and prepared to confront Cassie and meet her family. As he approached the door, he stepped on the small front porch nearly stepping on a cat that appeared from nowhere. The seemingly apparent stray attempted to jump on his leg and as he tried to avoid the cat, he almost stepped on the creature again. He was determined not to injure the tiny creature but his desperate movements caused him to lose his balance. He accidentally leaned on the doorbell multiple times while he attempted to regain his footing not wanting to fall and damage the beautiful bouquet he wanted to present to Cassie.

The sound of the extended doorbell ring interrupted their conversation about Jaquan.

"Damn, you've talked him up.", fussed Gina, "Listen to him pressing my doorbell like that. He gets on my nerves with that."

"Good, I'm glad he's here. He'll be here when Cassie arrives.", smirked Michell as he strutted to answer the door.

"Oh Lord! Did you invite him?", demanded Gloria.

Mitchell smiled and refused to respond while opening the door. He swung the door open without checking the peephole since he knew Jaquan's calling card.

"Come on in Ja …", Mitchell paused.

The tiny cat darted inside its family home after its daily morning outdoor adventure. Mitchell stared at the tall specimen at the doorway; he assumed that the white man with roses had to be Guy. He had no idea that Guy had such a commanding stature as he looked up to the semi-stranger. Cassie did have a type, thought Mitchell.

"Hello, sorry about leaning on your doorbell. I was trying not to step on that little guy.", Guy informed as he extended his hand, "I'm KC Guy Staton III."

Mitchell shook Guy's hand but was still speechless as he fully took in Cassie's muscle-bound fiancé.

"May I come inside?", asked Guy.

"Move and let the man inside!", shouted Gina.

"Of course, Guy; come in.", Mitchell replied as his thoughts became cohesive again, "I'm Mitchell, Cassie's father. The one yelling at me is Gina, Cassie's mother and the one sitting on the sofa is my sister-in-law, Gloria. She happened to marry a Williams from another branch."

Mitchell chuckled nervously as he observed Guy. Guy entered the cozy 1,500 square feet home and approached his soon-to-be mother-in-law to offer a hug. He quickly glanced around and noticed family pictures of Cassie with her parents; the pictures ranged from childhood to her college graduation. There were numerous trophies on the fireplace mantle that were probably the product of Cassie's successful academic career. It was obvious to Guy that they were doting parents and were very proud of her accomplishments. Gloria smiled and stood to greet him as she would not be left out. She initiated a hug from the strong young man and embraced him to welcome him into the family.

"So, Guy what brings you to the city?", questioned Mitchell with his arms crossed.

Guy was about to speak when Gina interrupted to scold her husband.

"To accept our daughter's apology. What else could it be?", Gina advised.

"That's only partially true. Cassie's not solely to blame for our break-up.", Guy admitted.

"Honey, have a seat and make yourself at home.", insisted Gina, and then her attention shifted to her husband, "Mitch, can I see you in the kitchen?"

"Yes, honey ...", Mitchell obliged.

He meekly followed his wife to the kitchen where he was sure he would receive a few stern words. They had barely entered the kitchen before Gina started fussing at her husband.

"I didn't care for your posture when you were speaking to Guy.", Gina admitted.

"I don't know what you mean. I was just standing my ground, man-to-man, and asked a question.", informed Mitchell, "Can't I ask a man to explain why he came to *my* house?"

"Let it have been Jaquan and it would have been a different story- high fives and fist pumps.", accused Gina.

"I need to tell Jaquan to get over here fast!", Mitchell blurted.

"No, the hell you don't! Leave that con artist right where he is. That one out there ...", Gina paused to point," That one out there is the real deal with a net worth of 700 million dollars."

Mitchell's entire demeanor changed as his eyes bucked in surprise.

"Why are you just standing there? Go offer the man something to drink.", Mitchell insisted.

Mitchell nudged Gina from the kitchen. He shuffled his feet behind her as they hurried back to the living room to attend to their future son-in-law.

Before Gina could open her mouth to offer anything to Guy, Mitchell took over and began speaking to him.

"Son, can I offer something to drink or would you like some of the catfish I'm about to fry up?", offered Mitchell.

"No thank you, sir. I really need to see Cassie. Would you let her know I'm here.", Guy informed.

"Sweetie, Cassie doesn't live with us. I thought you somehow found out she was coming.", laughed Gina.

"No, I didn't. This was the address her former boss gave me.", Guy confessed, "So, she's coming here?"

"Yes, our girl will be here shortly.", informed Gloria.

"Mitch, maybe you should start cooking that fish and we'll put the card game on hold.", suggested Gina.

"That's a good idea. Guy, just wait until you try my catfish. I know Cassie said you fry some pretty good fish, but wait until you taste mine.", Mitchell laughed as he headed to the kitchen.

Guy smiled at the surprising change in Mitchell's attitude. If only he could have heard Mrs. Williams check her husband; it must have been a powerful speech, thought Guy. Gina and Gloria talked to Guy to continue easing the tension that Mitchell had created earlier. Just as the three were laughing at some of the stories Guy shared from his chance encounters with Cassie, the doorbell rang multiple times. Gina immediately stopped laughing and her expression became tense, angry, and flushed.

"That better not be Jaquan!", growled Gina.

She purposely said it loud enough for her husband to hear from the kitchen. Mitchell dashed from the kitchen as he heard Jaquan's signature doorbell ringtone and instantly regretted telling Jaquan that Cassie would be over. Jaquan laid on the doorbell more as it seemed to take Cassie's parents longer to answer than normal. Mitchell opened the door and attempted to tell Jaquan to abort the plan, but Jaquan dodged Mitchell's hand and arrogantly entered the house.

"Thanks, Mitch, for looking out for your boy! This gave me an excuse to style and profile in my new Corvette.", chuckled Jaquan.

Jaquan stumbled over his next words and was unable to speak. His body became immobilized when he noticed Guy cozying up to the Williams family in the living room. Guy stood and the two six-feet-4-inch framed men stood at odds. Guy set the bouquet on the chair and clinched his fist daring Jaquan to say another word or take another step forward. Jaquan nervously stared at the women and looked to Mitchell for support and an explanation. Mitchell approached the young man to whisper that he should leave but before Mitchell could utter the words, Jaquan heeded Guy's warning and began walking backward toward the entrance.

"Jaquan, should I tell Cassie that you stopped by?", Mitchell nervously questioned.

"Naw, I'm good.", Jaquan whispered.

Cassie pulled her metallic grey Mercedes Maybach into her parents' driveway. She was very curious about the limousine parked in front of their home. She was eager to ask her parents if they saw where the visitor had gone and to whose house. Unlike Cassie, Princess became agitated and started barking as if she knew the person who had arrived by the luxury ride.

Jaquan heard a vehicle pull up outside and decided it was time to depart to spare himself more embarrassment. Consequently, his nod to Guy was adversarial; but it acknowledged Guy's dominance and he exited the home. As he walked down the walkway, Cassie's eyes were drawn away from the limousine when she noticed her ex-boyfriend leave her parents' house. She was furious that he had the nerve to come to her parents' home. She was tempted to release Princess' leash and allow the barking dog to attack him. He stopped to see what bullshit she was going to say.

"What the fuck are you doing here?", demanded Cassie., "Quiet girl; so, I can hear the lie!"

She was annoyed that he would come uninvited and even more so that he was showboating on top of it in a limousine knowing he couldn't afford the gas it took to fill it.

"Take that up with your daddy!", snarled Jaquan, "I ain't got time for this shit. It's too much tits and pussy out here for me to waste any more time on you."

Jaquan stormed past his once-upon-a-time lover without looking her in the eyes.

"You're right hoe. Go and find a broke dumb ass bitch to fool, with your broke ass.", Cassie retaliated.

Cassie was pissed with her father for once again putting his nose in her business. She stormed up the steps and used her key to open the door. Mitchell had not yet returned to the kitchen when Cassie opened it and saw him in the small foyer. She entered and immediately started yelling her frustrations at her father, the first and only person to whom her eyes were drawn. However, Princess saw and smelled someone she had missed and didn't have time to stick around in the foyer. She quickly darted into the living room causing Mitchell to stumble. He quickly regained his footing and turned to approach Cassie with a welcoming smile that soon turned to bewilderment.

"Daddy, what the fuck!", cried Cassie, "Why would you invite that loser here? That's the last thing I need right now. Daddy, you know how much I miss Guy!"

Mitchell thought she was calling Guy a loser, but he soon realized she must have run into Jaquan on her way in. His bewilderment turned to happiness because the one person in the world who made his angel happy was sitting in the other room.

"Daddy, why are you smiling like that? Didn't you hear me?", questioned a concerned Cassie.

"Cassie.", called Guy as he stood gently nudging Princess away, "I'm here baby."

Cassie turned to face the entrance to the living room and then her anger and tears slipped away as her eyes devoured Guy's tall frame. She ignored her ego, fears, and pretense and ran to his arms; she didn't have to be the poster girl for a strong black woman. At that moment, she only wanted to be Guy's girl. Guy lifted Cassie and she wrapped her legs around his torso. He held her tightly as their lips devoured the other's.

"Please forgive me, Cowboy.", begged Cassie.

"There is no need. I should be asking you to forgive me. If I had been honest about who I was, none of this would have ever happened.", Guy confessed.

"You're right none of it would have happened because I would never have dated you. So, things happened how they were supposed to.", Cassie rationalized, "I wouldn't have it any other way. I love you so much. I'm so glad you're here."

"I'll never leave your side again.", promised Guy.

Cassie's parents and aunt blushed as they witnessed the abandonment of the two lovers who had set all modesty aside. Normally Gloria would be very uncomfortable with public displays of affection, but she was thrilled over the moon that her niece had finally found true love.

"Thank you, Lord.", whispered Gloria.

Gina decided she would remind the two lovers that they were not alone.

"This is perfect. You both can sit and eat dinner with us. How does that sound?", asked Gina.

Guy looked at Cassie for her response.

"That's up to Cassie. We can stay here and eat or hop on my jet and head home.", Guy explained.

Mitchell mumbled the word jet in astonishment as his wide eyes looked at Gina who only nodded at her husband as if to say, I told you so.

"Let's go home.", squealed Cassie as she hugged Guy tightly.

"Well family, the Queen has spoken.", chuckled Guy.

Cassie picked up her purse and was about to take her bouquet with her when Guy touched her hand to stop her.

"You can leave those with your mother; there's more where those came from.", instructed Guy.

"What about her things and her car?", questioned Gina.

"Cassie can buy what she needs when we get home. And I'll send movers later to pack up anything she wants from her condo. I'll have her car shipped down if she wants. Hell, she can leave it here and buy a new one.", Guy informed.

"Well ... Daddy, you always tell me how much you love my car.", smiled Cassie.

Cassie winked and then handed her car keys to her father. Mitchell's mouth gaped as he accepted the keys. He was just as excited for Cassie's new life as she was. Gina and Gloria giggled with excitement for Cassie and Gina playfully tapped Mitchell on his shoulder.

Cassie wrapped her arm around Guy's waist and walked to the front door alongside her man with Princess leading the way. The pair bid everyone goodbye and walked outside to the limousine, where just as he had promised more flowers awaited her inside the plush luxury vehicle. The beautiful red roses were placed throughout, more than she had ever thought she would receive from a man. The combination of the fragrance and Guy's presence was intoxicating; she could scarcely think or focus. Guy notified the driver to return to the airport. Afterward, he popped the bottle of champagne causing Princess to bark as she waited attentively to see what would happen next while Guy filled their glasses for a toast.

"Cassie, every moment I look upon your face, you take my breath away. I knew from the first moment I saw you that I wanted you in my life.", confessed Guy.

For Cassie, listening to him was like watching a romantic love scene from a movie; what woman wouldn't be enthralled by his words?

"Oh, Cowboy, you have changed my life in so many ways ...", Cassie hesitated.

She fought back tears of joy as she cautiously sipped the champagne and rested her free hand on her flat stomach. Before she could swallow the small sip, Guy kissed her passionately as he sucked the remnants of champagne from her mouth. Her giggles filled the limousine for the entire ride to the airport as they seemed to arrive in no time. Guy refused to wait for the driver to open the door for either of them as he exited and aided Cassie from the vehicle. Then effortlessly, he lifted Cassie and walked toward the portable stairs. Princess insisted on being the leader and ran ahead leaving Guy in her dust as he carried Cassie up the stairs to board the plane.

"Cowboy, please be careful ...", insisted Cassie.

Guy had never seen her look so nervous before.

"We can't have you putting Pink Rose's first grandbaby in harm's way.", whispered Cassie.

"Oh ... a little princess?", Guy's smile broadened as he questioned her.

Guy was shocked by the news and he could not hide his boy-like excitement. He slowed his jog up the stairs to a walk as he boarded the plane with his family in his arms. He set her down in a seat and then he sat beside her.

"You know it could be a little cowboy.", laughed Cassie.

"Or twins! Daddy's little princess and Mommy's little cowboy.", chuckled Guy.

"Don't manifest that. I can only handle one at a time.", teased Cassie.

"Trust me, Ma will wait on you hand and foot and spoil the hell out of our kids.", laughed Guy.

"I can't even imagine her waiting on me hand and foot. Shit! I'd like to see that bitch do that! No offense.", laughed Cassie.

"None taken. I do love two strong bitches.", Guy's laughter roared.

"You're lucky I love you.", Cassie teased.

She playfully punched his stomach and then began to kiss every inch of his face until Guy took control of the situation by turning those playful kisses into passionate ones. His hands touched every inch of her as he slid his hands under her dress. Cassie knew exactly what her cowboy wanted and needed; she began unbuckling his belt and pants.

"Yeah, take that cock out and ride it.", panted Guy.

"Naw baby, a cock is a bird. This ...", Cassie said as she gripped his manhood, "This Is a dick big as fuck!"

Guy loved her use of urban vernacular to describe things, but his laughter was short-lived as pleasure and desire replaced it as she skillfully straddled his manhood. The flight back to Mississippi consisted of one passionate romp after another as laughter and groans filled the small aircraft.

Chapter 14

Tim was extremely annoyed that Guy had flown to Detroit to win Cassie back. He had stopped by Staton Farms the day Guy left and Henry was overjoyed to inform him that Guy had listened to him and his mother. Tim was shocked that Ms. Rose had agreed with the plan; Cassie must have witching powers to have convinced Ms. Rose to accept her. Tim rushed to Pete's office hoping that Pete saw things from his perspective and if not, he hoped to recruit Pete. Perhaps Tim could persuade Pete to talk some sense into their mutual friend. Tim entered the local Sheriff's office rushing past the officers and ignoring their greetings, and then Tim barged through Pete's office door unannounced. The action alarmed Pete causing him to place his hand on his pistol holster.

"Don't get yourself shot in here.", chuckled Pete, "I'm not used to people forcing their way into my office."

"Hey, Pete I'm sorry for that.", Tim apologized, "I'm just concerned about Guy."

"What about him? Did something else happen at the farm?", inquired Pete.

"Fuck the farm!", Tim growled, "I'm talking about Guy being a dumb ass."

"A dumb ass?", Pete questioned.

Pete repositioned himself in his chair preparing to listen to his friend disclose whatever Guy had done to worry him. He had not seen Tim this angry about anything since his early teen years.

"What did he do?", Pete asked.

"He flew to Detroit to bring that bitch back home.", Tim insulted.

"Bitch? Wait a minute. There's no need to speak of Cassie like that.", Pete defended, "He loves her, and I as well as his mother encouraged him to go."

"So, Cassie's gotten to you too.", alleged Tim, "I don't know why everyone but me is so willing to accept her in his life. She is a liar. Once a liar, always a liar. I wouldn't trust her!"

"Good thing she's not in a relationship with you", Pete responded, "I think your energy would be better placed on working things out with your own woman."

"That fucker!", shouted Tim, "So, Trudie is confiding in you nowadays?"

"Reel it back, brother.", Pete cautioned, "You know our wives are friends and my wife tells me everything. I don't know what has gotten into you lately, but maybe you need to see a therapist like when your dad died ..."

"Wow!", Tim ranted, "Trudie strikes again. I see I'm the only one who really cares for *our* friend."

"I love Guy like a brother, but I know when to focus on my own shit, my woman. I think you should learn to do the same.", Pete advised.

"Well fuck it. I'll just have to figure something else out.", Tim snarled.

Pete did not know how to respond to that and didn't understand why Tim would be so upset about a decision Guy made for his own life. However, Pete did not have an opportunity to say anything before Tim stormed out and slammed the office door breaking a hinge. Tim's uncharacteristic actions startled the officers congregating and sitting near Pete's office. One of the deputies rushed inside Pete's office to check on his superior officer.

"Sheriff, is everything okay?", asked the deputy.

"The fuck if I know.", Pete confessed, "Call Buddy to fix the hinge and get back to work."

"Yes sir.", agreed the deputy.

Tim was furious with Pete; he would add Pete to the list of folks with whom he was fed up. Nothing seemed to be going as planned for him. His wife was leaving him, his business had taken a surprising downturn, and his old buried feelings were rearing their ugly heads. His thoughts were just as muddled as they had been decades ago when his father died. He felt his father's death was a senseless one at the hands of a man who thought his wealth entitled him to take anything he wanted even if it was another man's wife.

Rage filled Tim's heart and mind causing him to recklessly drive his sports car at high speed on the country roads as he drove aimlessly around the countryside. His mind convinced him that the only thing left to do was get his revenge on the family of the man, the murderer, since the angel of death had already claimed him.

The weeks following Cassie and Guy's return to Mississippi were blissful for the couple and exciting news for everyone else. Cassie had never felt more at home and peaceful than the nights she slept in Guy's arms at the Staton mansion. She had been speechless when Pink hugged her and welcomed her home. She would never have guessed they could set aside their differences and focus on a common love. Guy couldn't wait to share the news of Cassie's pregnancy until their arrival that fateful day; instead, he called his mother immediately after arriving at the airport. Guy then proudly told Henry the news as the couple entered the Rolls Royce. Henry reacted as a doting soon-to-be-grandfather would; he hugged Cassie and Guy as if they were his children. Then just as abruptly he resumed his duties as driver and head butler and drove the couple home.

Cassie and Guy's unborn bundle of joy was the talk of the mansion and the farm. The head foreman, Chip, offered a tour of the farm and its operations; Pink Rose offered her a tour of the mansion and even Staton Holdings, Inc. corporate offices. Pink proudly introduced Cassie to the staff as they toured.

"I think you would be a great asset here. We could use someone as talented and driven to maintain and even elevate our interests.", suggested Pink.

Cassie nearly choked on her saliva as she tried to swallow and clear her throat.

"Pink, I …", paused Cassie.

"I don't mean to tell you what to do. I truly understand if you want to focus on our little one when he or she is born.", Pink apologized.

"No, I'm not offended, just more shocked than anything.", Cassie laughed, "To be honest, I hadn't thought that far into the future. I would love to be a stay-at-home mom because I know how great my childhood was for having one. But I am passionate about my work; success in the boardroom is an adrenaline rush. It's a special kind of high, you know, that's not easily understood unless a person experiences it."

"I completely understand.", laughed Pink, "You sound just like me when I was a young wife and mother. Unbelievable. Mama Staton watched over my children while I worked and helped build Staton Holdings, Inc. into what it is today. Without her, I would have been a miserable wife and a horrible mother; I probably would have taken my frustrations out on my babies and husband."

Cassie was speechless that Pink, such a stoic woman, felt vulnerable enough to share her story. As Guy had said they were cut from the same cloth and the more Cassie and Pink spent time together it became quite apparent to them both.

"Let's go for lunch. Did Guy ever take you to Colleen's Kitchen?", Pink asked.

"No, he never mentioned it.", Cassie responded.

"It's a little family-owned restaurant with the most delicious fried chicken, macaroni, and cheese.", Pink salivated, "I can taste it now."

Cassie and Pink Rose exited the building laughing like they had been close girlfriends for years. Both ladies were excited about the future; nothing was more exciting for them than an upcoming marriage and welcoming a new life to the world.

As the Staton clan became more of a united front, the conspirator fumed at his past failures of destroying the family. The conspirator was determined more than ever to hurt the *loving* family. He searched his shed frantically until he found the bullets for his rifle. However, he considered another plan when he remembered the other weapon he kept inside the house. He would take drastic measures into his own hands since the acquisitions company had backed out and refused to take any of his calls. He was on his own; if he wanted to see his childhood dream of revenge, it would have to be by his rifle. It was no longer enough for the conspirator to damage the Staton business; he was desperate to satisfy his heart's bloodthirst for that family.

It was time for the Staton family to pay for the sins of Guy KC Staton Jr., the bastard who killed his father and had an adulterous relationship with his mother. It was time that the town knew that the man they believed was a saint was a true devil who had caused him a lifetime of pain and sorrow. The gears of his mind churned and he realized that he should not kill Guy but take from him what mattered to him the most, those two bitches, thought the conspirator.

Despite hashing out part of the plan, the conspirator needed someone to cause a distraction on the farm to help him enact his plans. He decided to rent another car and drive into the small town of Grey Creek to find more poor saps in need of cash; there was one on every acre of the deprived town.

Guy had completed his morning chores and was feeling whole as he stood in the warm sunlight of Autumn; he said a silent prayer of thanksgiving for all his blessings. It was another gorgeous day on the farm and Guy couldn't be happier in his element and knowing that the two people he esteemed above all were getting along. Guy checked in on all the farm's operations and was overjoyed that the farm was flourishing despite the past attacks. After he exited the chicken farm, he noticed Pete approaching from his vehicle.

"Hey brother, I'm glad I caught you before you started grounds patrol on horseback.", Pete informed.

"Good thing, I was just headed to the stables. What's up?", Guy asked.

"I was hoping you could tell me.", chuckled Pete, "I don't know what is going on with Tim. I can only imagine how difficult a divorce might be but ..."

"Divorce! Tim and Trudie are getting a divorce?", Guy questioned.

"Yeah, I assumed you knew.", Pete admitted.

"Hell no. I've been hell-bent on getting my girl back. This is news to me.", Guy confessed, "When did he tell you?"

"He didn't; I heard it from my wife, who heard it from Trudie.", Pete informed, "Don't you find it weird that he isn't confiding in us anymore?"

"It's a little odd, but you've done that before too.", Guy reminded Pete.

Pete nodded in agreement.

"Yes, because it was a really rough patch coping with my father's death.", Pete admitted.

"But again, I had more important things to focus on. My girl for one and then there's Staton Farms.", Guy reminded, "Besides, Tim is a grown man who can handle his shit. If he can't then that's on him."

"Brother, that's the thing. He's not handling it well.", sighed Pete, "Carol, said he's been living a double life, a woman on the side, hours away from home, drinking, and only God knows what else."

"So, he's spiraling out of control like before.", determined Guy.

"Seems like it. The other day, he barged into my office looking like a crazed man. I almost shot his ass.", Pete fussed.

"I've been by his side once before during some very dark days and … I can't commit to that now. I have a wedding to plan and a baby on the way.", Guy explained.

"Congratulations!", Pete bellowed, "You're going to be Pappa Staton."

Pete shook Guy's hand and the two pulled each other in for a bear hug.

"Well, shit! I understand where you're coming from now.", laughed Pete, "I'll tell Carol she should stop gossiping or at least don't unload stuff on me."

"Exactly!", laughed Guy, "Did I tell you how my two girls are getting along?"

"No …", laughed Pete.

"Patrol with me and I'll tell you what the staff said.", chuckled Guy.

"Tell me now. I have an errand to run.", chuckled Pete.

The evening approached leaving the conspirator only a few more hours of daylight as he drove around the back woods of Grey Creek in search of someone to aid in his plans. He was desperate to end things that night and as his luck would have it, it did not take long for him to spot a group of young men who looked like they needed cash and were looking for trouble. He sized them up to be ripe for the picking and would factor in perfectly for his plan. He pulled alongside them to get their attention.

"Do you want to make some quick cash?", asked the conspirator.

"It all depends on the shit we have to do to get it.", voiced the leader.

"Nothing worse than you've probably already done.", sneered the conspirator.

The leader looked at his peers and nodded. They approached the car to hear the scheme. The conspirator explained the plan to the young men as they gathered closer to hear all the details. The men laughed and the leader tapped the car with his hand. He was excited about the payday that was just hours away. The conspirator handed an envelope stuffed with hundred-dollar bills to the leader. Then the conspirator informed the young men that he would leave more money at the drop-off point on Staton Farms for the men to split.

As the conspirator departed the young men, an evil satisfied grin spread from ear to ear; he would finally have revenge for his father's death and the miserable life that he experienced with a heartbroken mother. He shouted cheers of excitement as he banged his fists against the steering wheel. He would finally have the revenge he had craved since childhood.

The night sky's darkness cloaked the farm; evening hours had become Cassie's favorite time of the day. It was when she could have Guy all to herself. Cassie and Guy sat in front of the fireplace in the study. It was a cozy and romantic thing they did often as they experienced the cooler Autumn nights together. She teased him that they were like an old couple cuddled together as they discussed the activities of their respective day. Recently, their discussions focused more on the upcoming nuptials and the extensive guest list that grew daily.

"This is nice., Cowboy", Cassie whispered.

She snuggled against Guy's warm chest and he kissed her atop her head.

"Yes, it is.", sighed Guy, "This is the happiest I've ever been."

"Me too.", giggled Cassie, "Just think, soon we will learn the gender of our baby."

Just as Guy was about to respond, he received an urgent text message from Chip and a notification from the new security system. Pink Rose had received the same alerts before she rushed inside to discuss it with Guy.

"Did you get the security notifications?", questioned Pink Rose.

"Yeah, I did. What the fuck!", shouted Guy.

Cassie was confused that there would be trouble after the acquisition company swore that they were backing off.

"A group of men were seen on the property.", Pink Rose explained to Cassie.

"Not again … I don't understand.", Cassie cried.

"Honey, don't worry about this. I'll get it handled.", Guy promised.

Guy kissed Cassie's forehead as he stood to leave. Pink rushed over to the fireplace to retrieve the rifle above the mantle.

She quickly walked to the built-in bookshelf to grab a hollowed book that stored rifle bullets inside.

"Wait Guy!", shouted Pink Rose as she began to follow him.

"No, Ma. I'll take that and you stay here with Cassie.", Guy demanded.

"Okay, but how am I supposed to protect us if you take the rifle?", questioned Pink Rose.

"I'll have someone outside the main entrance, but I doubt that anyone will be that fucking stupid to enter our home.", insisted Guy.

Guy buttoned his shirt as he left the room. Pink Rose and Cassie hated the idea of them sitting and waiting aimlessly for updates; they wanted to be on the front lines. They refused to let him address the situation alone so they followed him outside the mansion. Henry joined the ladies as they rushed behind Guy outside the massive doors. So many things were pulling and fighting for Guy's attention from the ladies, to text messages, and calls. Everything was happening simultaneously; he had even received text messages from Pete and Tim. Guy text messaged Tim providing an update about the incident and Tim promised to watch over his mother and Cassie. Pete said he had already left for the farm after he received the security notification. After ensuring Cassie's and his mother's safety, Guy called Chip from his cell phone.

"Chip, saddle up my horse, yours, and one for Pete. I'll be there in a moment.", ordered Guy.

Guy attempted to get in his truck when Cassie tugged at his arm to stop him. Pink Rose was close behind Cassie begging Guy to wait.

"Ma, Cassie … please!", Guy said as he held up a finger to halt their requests, "What the fuck!", shouted Guy as he received more text messages.

Cassie leaned on Guy's shoulder to provide her support.

"Guy, you don't have to do things alone anymore. I'm here. This is my legacy now too, I'm going with you.", Cassie insisted.

"Cassie, stay here!", shouted Guy, "I will not let anything happen to you and our baby!"

Guy threw up his hand to stop her and to shut down the idea. The force and power in his usually gentle voice halted her tongue. She had never felt so protected and aroused by his commanding presence. Pink Rose observed Cassie; she recognized the look on Cassie's face. It was the same look of respect, passion, and love she gave KC Jr. whenever he took charge. Pink Rose would surrender to her husband's strength and his will. At that moment, Pink Rose realized Cassie truly respected and loved her son and he loved Cassie as well. Guy softened his gaze and tone as he continued to speak.

"Ladies, Tim said he's on his way. He'll look out for you both. Please go inside.", Guy instructed before hopping into his truck.

Guy sped off to meet Chip and Pete but he noticed Tim approaching. He honked his horn and waved at his old friend, but he was surprised that Tim made such good timing. However, he did not have time to waste by asking Tim how.

"Let's get you ladies inside and I'll sit with you.", Henry said.

"None sense. Henry, go ahead and retire for the evening. We will be fine. Besides Guy told us that Tim is going to join us. We will be perfectly fine.", Pink Rose reassured, "There's Tim now."

"As you wish, Mrs. Staton.", Henry said before entering the mansion.

Tim pulled up the circular drive and parked in front of the main entrance. He exited the vehicle carrying a rifle. Cassie noticed Tim was wearing gloves, but it didn't seem cold enough.

"Why are you wearing gloves?", Cassie questioned.

Pink Rose and Tim laughed at her question.

"They are hunting gloves. They give me a better grip for the rifle.", Tim advised, "Let's get inside. We don't need to take any unnecessary chances."

Tim scanned the area before closing the door; he didn't notice anyone nearby. Therefore, he reassured the ladies as they entered. The situation was quite different for the search party. The bright moonlight aided the hunt as Guy, Chip, and Pete patrolled the grounds; they noticed another group of young men. The group instantly split up and began fleeing the area when the patrol party shined flashlights at them. The three chased the larger group, Guy did not want them to split up. He planned to question the guys once caught and he would have the police to round up the others later with the evidence he would gather. Guy, Chip, and Pete surrounded four of the men and pulled their rifles on them.

"What the fuck are you doing on my land?", Guy demanded.

"Hey brother, we were just trying to find a place to have a few beers and smoke weed.", the leader lied as he flashed a backpack with beers inside.

"Don't come the fuck back or your ass and my rifle will have an introduction.", yelled Guy.

The young men ran off swearing that they would never return.

"Boys, I'm going to head back to the house first to check on my girls, then I'll meet you back at the office to complete the paperwork for the police and security reports.", Guy informed.

The men nodded and rode off to the office and Guy headed in the opposite direction to the mansion. He wanted to reassure the women in person that everything was okay before he completed the paperwork.

The ladies hesitated to enter the family room when they noticed Tim looking out a window. He insisted that the ladies continue walking. He gazed through the windows to ensure no one lurked in the shadows. The three entered the family room and Tim closed the doors behind them; he locked them to prevent anyone from entering. Tim set the rifle on the floor and leaned it against the sofa.

"I don't understand why this is happening again.", Cassie insisted, "Did you ever have problems like this before my old company harassed you?"

"Not at all.", Pink Rose responded, "We don't have any enemies. No one would want to hurt us like this."

"Are you sure about that Ms. Rose?", Tim questioned.

Pink Rose looked shocked that Tim would even suggest such a thing. However, Tim's comment reminded Cassie of something Guy told her months back; that the family had a good history depending on who you questioned. Tim noticed Cassie's expression of acknowledgment.

"So, Guy must have told you.", Tim assumed.

Cassie was very confused by Tim's words and intentions.

"No, he just said that the reputation of the family depended on who you spoke to.", Cassie admitted.

"This family has lots of secrets ...", Tim began.

"This is not the time for that.", Pink Rose insisted.

"Why not? She should know what type of family she's marrying into. What legacy is growing in her belly.", laughed Tim.

225

"This is ridiculous. I need a drink.", Pink Rose fussed.

"People think, KC Jr. was a saint, but he was a devil ...", Tim began.

"Not that shit ...", Pink Rose exclaimed as she slammed the whiskey bottle on the console table.

"It's the truth ... if he hadn't fucked my mother, I would have a family today.", Tim shouted.

"What?", whispered Cassie.

"Pay him no mind. His story is from the mind of a child who didn't know what was going on.", Pink Rose yelled.

"My father made sure I knew exactly what was going on. He told me how your husband wanted my mother.", Tim ranted.

"Your *father* was a drunk, who my *husband* pitied and kept him employed on the farm so you and your mother wouldn't starve to death.", shouted Pink Rose, "In fact, my husband was a better father to you than your own ever was!"

"Now there's the bitch we all know! My father was a good man, a hardworking man...", Tim barked.

"Yeah, when he wasn't drunk, but God knows he had more drunk days than sober. Just ask your ma; he was an angry drunk and beat her ass every time a bottle touched his lips.", shouted Pink Rose.

"My father only beat her because of her relationship with KC. I guess you were too busy running the corporate offices, to know your husband was whoring around with my mother during work hours.", Tim spat, "The day my father died he walked in on your husband and my mother..."

"No, little boy! KC was going to send you two away to her family up North so she could start over.", shouted Pink Rose, "But

226

your drunk pappy tried to shoot my husband and he learned that day that threatening a Staton will get you killed."

"You can believe what you want, but I know the womanizer your husband was.", Tim accused, "He thought his wealth entitled him to whatever he wanted, much like you and Guy."

Tim removed a gun from his jacket pocket; it was equipped with a silencer and pointed it at the two women. Cassie had never seen such evil eyes; the man she thought she knew was gone or possessed by something evil. Her eyes searched for any nearby weapon as did Pink Rose. Pink Rose remembered the rifle leaning against the sofa. She quickly reached for it when Tim eyed his watch.

"Put the gun down. I'm a much better shot than you.", Pink Rose warned.

"True, good thing I didn't add any bullets.", laughed Tim, "I'm not stupid bitch. I've been playing you for months. I was the one helping RQ and the mastermind behind the attacks."

"You? Please, … Tim don't do this. It won't change the past.", pleaded Pink Rose.

"It will give me years of pleasure knowing I killed the two bitches Guy can't live without.", laughed Tim, "He'll be a broken man and probably will lose everything his great-great-grandpappy created. Or is it great-great-great-grandpappy?"

Tim moved the gun's aim right and left as if trying to decide who would be first. Cassie began yelling at Tim and she begged him to think of his wife and children.

"Fuck her and those kids. She's leaving me already.", laughed Tim, "And my business is taking a nose dive. I really don't have much to lose."

Guy pulled up behind Tim's car and parked. He grabbed the rifle to return it to the mantle; it had been years since it had been fired. He was racking his brain trying to figure out why this was happening. They had never had issues with the locals disrespecting their land before. He wondered if this was just the start of what future operations would have to manage.

When Guy entered the mansion and approached the closed doors to the family room, he heard arguing and Pink begging someone to spare Cassie and the baby. He quickly approached the doors to find them locked. He was going crazy with worry and imagining horrific things happening to Cassie and their unborn child. Cassie was his life and motivation for everything he did or thought to do. His fury blinded him and fueled his actions as he kicked in the door. He did not see who was holding the gun, only that someone was pointing the gun at the love of his life and if she died, he died. Guy immediately pulled the trigger aiming the rifle at the man's chest.

The sound of the gunshots scared both Pink Rose and Cassie; as the bullet from Guy's gun blasted Tim in the chest, Tim's gun released a shot that hit the wall behind the frightened women. Guy ran to Cassie to check on her.

"Did he hurt you?", asked Guy.

"No, the baby and I are fine.", Cassie informed.

"Ma?", asked Guy.

'I'm fine. I just can't believe Tim was behind all the attacks.", Pink Rose admitted.

"Tim?", questioned Guy.

It was the first time that he had looked at the gunman's face and his heart sank. Not only had he shot and killed his childhood friend, but that friend had been willing to hurt those he held closest to his heart.

"I know Pooh Bear.", Pink Rose comforted.

Pink hugged him from the side providing the comfort she knew he needed. Neither she nor Guy had known that Tim had harbored so much hatred for them all those years. Pink Rose repeated the details of the evening to Guy and told him the horrible things that Tim had believed about KC Jr. and confessed his part in the attacks to them while he had held them captive.

Guy listened to his mother and Cassie talk about what happened as if they were retelling a movie. They seemed unaffected by their experience. In contrast, Guy was in shock and he sat down on the sofa to hide that his legs were shaking; he was still nervous despite that threat lying dead on the floor.

"I guess I really do love two tough bitches.", chuckled Guy in a whisper as he ran his hands through his long mane.

"Yes, you do.", laughed Pink, "We really are a lot alike."

The ladies revisited an old discussion about Cassie's future with the family business as if nothing life-threatening had occurred. They continued the conversation as they approached the broken door to exit the room. Guy turned sideways on the sofa to watch the ladies leave; he was in disbelief that the ladies were not giving Tim any more thought.

"Staton Holdings Inc. could really use you to head up one of our departments.", Pink Rose admitted.

"That sounds very tempting, but after all this, I need to focus on cranking out this little Staton first.", laughed Cassie.

The two women walked arm in arm as they entered the foyer.

"Girls, the police will need statements from you.", Guy reminded.

The ladies' laughter drowned out Guy's words as the two walked the great halls of Staton Manor.